THE MEDICI KILLER

A Thrilling Crime Mystery

ARIEL SANDERS

Copyright © 2025 by ARIEL SANDERS
All rights reserved.

No part of this book may be reproduced, stored in a retrieval system, or transmitted in any form or by any means—electronic, mechanical, photocopying, recording, or otherwise—without the prior written permission of the publisher, except in the case of brief quotations used in reviews.

This book is intended for entertainment purposes only. While every effort has been made to ensure accuracy, the author and publisher make no representations or warranties regarding the completeness, accuracy, or reliability of the information contained within. The reader assumes full responsibility for their interpretation and application of any content in this book.

Index

Chapter 1 The Discovery	5
Chapter 2 The Medici Court	9
Chapter 3 The First Warning	16
Chapter 4 The Masked Killer Strikes Again	27
Chapter 5 The Investigation Begins	36
Chapter 6 The Medici Ball	48
Chapter 7 The Family Crypt	56
Chapter 8 The Artisan's Workshop	66
Chapter 9 The Conspiracy Unravels	76
Chapter 10 Trap at the Cathedral	90
Chapter 11 Isabella's Discovery	100
Epilogue Blood and Legacy	110

SPECIAL BONUS

Want this Bonus Ebook for *free*?

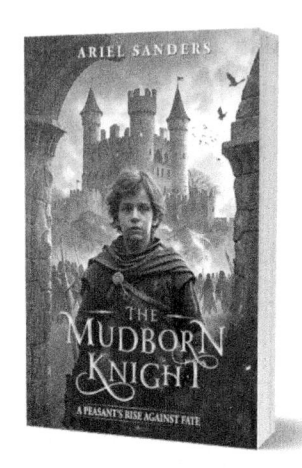

SCAN W/ YOUR CAMERA TO DOWNLOAD THE EBOOK!

SCAN ME

Chapter 1
The Discovery

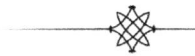

The body lay twisted in the narrow alley, blood pooling beneath it like spilled wine on the cobblestones. Dawn's pale fingers had just begun to creep over Florence's skyline when the baker's boy stumbled upon it—a nobleman, by the cut of his doublet, though the face was now unrecognizable. The throat had been opened with such precision that the head lolled backward at an impossible angle, held to the torso by mere threads of sinew.

Gian Lorenzo Pazzi had been a man of considerable girth in life. In death, he seemed deflated, as though whatever essence had animated him had been thoroughly drained away. His rings remained on his fingers, his purse still heavy with florins at his belt. This was no common thievery.

By mid-morning, a crowd had gathered at the edges of the scene, held back by the city guards who had cordoned off the alleyway. The body lay less than fifty paces from the imposing facade of the Medici palace, a fact not lost on the whispering onlookers.

Captain Nico della Torre knelt beside the corpse, his weathered face betraying nothing as he examined the wounds. Twenty years in service to Florence's militia had hardened him to the sight of violent death, but something about this killing disturbed him deeply. The cuts were too clean, too deliberate. Five precise punctures formed a pattern across the man's chest, each penetrating to exactly the same depth.

"A stiletto," he murmured to his lieutenant. "Thin-bladed. The work of someone who understands anatomy." His thick fingers traced the air above the wounds, connecting them mentally. "See how they form a perfect pentagon?"

What caught della Torre's eye next sent a chill through his battle-hardened frame. Placed delicately on the dead man's forehead, as if in grotesque benediction, lay a single crimson feather. Not haphazardly fallen there, but positioned with deliberate care.

"Collect that," he ordered, pointing to the feather. "And search the area thoroughly."

As the guards began their work, a commotion at the edge of the crowd drew della Torre's attention. The people parted like the sea before Moses as a procession of richly dressed men approached, led by a figure whose mere presence commanded deference.

Lorenzo de' Medici—called "Il Magnifico" by admirers and enemies alike—surveyed the scene with calculated detachment. Though not particularly tall or imposing physically, power emanated from him like heat from a forge. His hooded eyes missed nothing.

"Captain," Lorenzo acknowledged della Torre with a slight nod. "What tragedy visits our fair city this morning?"

Before della Torre could answer, one of Lorenzo's companions stepped forward and gasped. "God in heaven, it's Pazzi!"

Lorenzo's expression darkened momentarily before returning to careful neutrality. "Gian Lorenzo Pazzi? You're certain?"

"Yes, my lord. We dined together just three nights past at the Cavalcanti banquet."

A murmur rippled through both the noble contingent and the common onlookers. The Pazzi family, while not as powerful as the Medici, were still among Florence's elite. This was no ordinary murder; it was a message.

Lorenzo stepped closer, heedless of the blood soaking into the hem of his expensive robe. He studied the corpse with the same analytical eye he might apply to a ledger or a political treaty.

"These wounds," he said quietly to della Torre. "They seem... deliberate."

The captain nodded. "And this was left upon him." He held up the crimson feather, now carefully wrapped in linen.

Something flashed in Lorenzo's eyes—recognition? Alarm? It vanished too quickly for della Torre to be certain.

"I want this matter resolved swiftly, Captain," Lorenzo said, his voice carrying the unmistakable weight of command. "Whoever has done this has struck at the heart of Florence's peace. Find them."

As Lorenzo turned to leave, della Torre noticed that one member of his entourage lingered, staring at the body with an intensity that bordered on fascination rather than horror. A young woman, perhaps twenty years of age, dressed in the height of Florentine fashion but with a severity unusual for her youth. Her dark eyes seemed to be memorizing every detail of the grisly tableau.

"Lady Isabella," della Torre called out, recognizing Lorenzo's niece. "You should not trouble yourself with such unpleasantness."

Isabella de' Medici straightened, meeting the captain's gaze with unexpected directness. "Knowledge is never unpleasant, Captain, merely necessary or unnecessary. I find this knowledge quite necessary."

With that cryptic statement, she turned and followed her uncle, the crimson feather's twin tucked discreetly into her sleeve—snatched from the ground where it had fallen unnoticed by the guards. As she walked away, her mind raced with questions.

Why would the killer leave two feathers? Was the second meant to be found, or had it been dropped accidentally? And why did her uncle's face flash with recognition at the sight of the first?

By midday, news of the murder had spread throughout Florence like wildfire. By evening, it had transformed into something more potent: fear. For the nobility of Florence understood what the common folk did not—that Gian Lorenzo Pazzi had been one of Lorenzo de' Medici's most faithful supporters in the banking guild. This was no random killing. This was a challenge to Medici authority itself.

And as night fell over the city, in a small, candlelit workshop far from the grandeur of the palazzos, gloved hands carefully applied gold leaf to a mask of exquisite craftsmanship—a mask designed not for Carnival revelry, but for a very different kind of performance.

Chapter 2
The Medici Court

---※---

The great hall of the Palazzo Medici thrummed with activity despite the early hour. Courtiers and petitioners hovered in clusters, their voices a carefully modulated hum that rose and fell like the tide. Servants glided between groups, offering refreshments from silver trays. Artists and scholars congregated near the windows, where the morning light best served their discussions of perspective and proportion.

At the center of this carefully orchestrated chaos sat Lorenzo de' Medici, receiving supplicants from a chair that—while deliberately not throne-like—nevertheless conveyed absolute authority. His secretary stood at his right hand, while various advisors orbited nearby, ready to offer counsel when summoned.

"The guild of wool merchants requests a reduction in the export tax," the secretary murmured, presenting a sealed document.

Lorenzo's fingers drummed thoughtfully on the arm of his chair. "Tell them I'll consider it after they've made their promised contribution to the Duomo's new baptistery doors." His voice was pitched perfectly—loud enough for nearby courtiers to hear and spread word of his patronage, soft enough to maintain the illusion of private deliberation.

Such was the dance of power in Florence, where banking wealth and artistic patronage were the twin pillars of Medici influence. Lorenzo had elevated this dance to an art form. Unlike his grandfather Cosimo, who accumulated power through shrewd banking, or his father Piero, who maintained it through careful alliances, Lorenzo wielded influence through culture. He made

Florence the envy of the world, and in doing so, made himself indispensable to the city's identity.

From her position at the periphery of the hall, Isabella de' Medici observed her uncle with calculating admiration. At twenty-two, she possessed the famous Medici intellect in full measure, yet found herself constrained by the limitations of her sex. While Lorenzo's son Piero was being groomed for leadership despite his mediocre mind, Isabella's brilliant political insights were confined to private journals and whispered suggestions.

"He's refused the wool merchants again," came a voice at her elbow. Niccolò Machiavelli, barely twenty himself but already making a name in diplomatic circles, had a talent for appearing silently at opportune moments.

Isabella didn't turn. "They overreached. The timing is poor with the Pazzi murder unsettling the banking community."

"Speaking of which," Niccolò lowered his voice further, "there are whispers that the Pazzi family blames Lorenzo for failing to protect their kinsman."

"Convenient whispers for those who would drive a wedge between Florence's leading families." Isabella finally faced the young diplomat. "What else have you heard?"

Machiavelli's thin lips curved in a smile that never reached his eyes. "That depends on what information you might exchange. Your cousin Giulio was seen leaving the archbishop's residence well after midnight. Strange hours for a man supposedly devoted to secular pursuits."

Isabella filed this away for future consideration. Her cousin Giulio, illegitimate son of Lorenzo's murdered brother, moved in shadows even within the Medici inner circle. His ambitions were as obvious as they were dangerous.

"The second feather," she said softly, "was not mentioned in any official report of the murder."

Machiavelli's eyebrows rose fractionally—the closest he came to expressing surprise. "Most interesting. An oversight? Or deliberate omission?"

Their exchange was interrupted by a commotion at the hall's entrance. The crowd parted to reveal Cardinal Riario, nephew of Pope Sixtus IV and no friend to the Medici. His arrival unannounced was itself a minor provocation.

Lorenzo rose smoothly, his face betraying nothing as he extended his hands to the Cardinal. "Your Eminence honors our humble home. Had we known of your visit, we would have prepared a welcome befitting your station."

The Cardinal's smile was a thin slash across his ascetic face. "Some matters cannot wait on ceremony, Magnifico. I come bearing condolences from His Holiness for the unfortunate death of Signor Pazzi." The emphasis he placed on "unfortunate" carried unmistakable insinuation.

"Most generous of His Holiness," Lorenzo replied evenly, "though one might wonder why a simple banker's death warrants papal attention."

The exchange continued in this vein—courteous words laden with barbed subtexts—while Isabella drifted closer, observing the Cardinal's entourage. Her attention fixed on a figure half-hidden behind the clerical retinue: a man in his thirties, dressed simply but in fabrics no common man could afford. His face was memorable for its symmetry, handsome in a severe way, with eyes that seemed to absorb light rather than reflect it.

He caught her staring and held her gaze with unsettling intensity. Then, shockingly, he winked—a gesture so inappropriate in the formal setting that Isabella nearly gasped. Before she could react further, he had melted away into the crowd.

"Who was that man?" she demanded of Machiavelli, but the young diplomat merely shrugged.

"A new player on the board, it seems. How interesting that he caught your attention among so many more obvious threats."

Across the hall, Lorenzo was concluding his verbal fencing match with the Cardinal. "...and you may assure His Holiness that Florence remains devoted to the Church, even as we pursue our own civic destiny."

"His Holiness prays for Florence daily," the Cardinal replied. "Especially that its leaders might recognize the difference between civic destiny and unchecked ambition." With a slight bow that bordered on insulting, he turned to leave.

As the Cardinal's party departed, Lorenzo summoned his inner circle with a subtle gesture. They converged on him like planets to a sun: Poliziano, the brilliant humanist scholar; Botticelli, whose paintings glorified the Medici even as they depicted classical gods; Giulio de' Medici, whose clerical connections provided invaluable intelligence from Rome; and Michelozzi, Lorenzo's personal secretary and keeper of the family's darkest secrets.

Isabella moved to join them but was intercepted by her aunt Clarice, Lorenzo's wife. "Your uncle meets with his advisors, child. We have matters of our own to discuss."

Clarice Orsini, Roman-born and never fully accepted by Florentine society despite two decades of marriage to Lorenzo, ruled the domestic sphere of the Medici household with iron determination. She guided Isabella to a window alcove where they could speak privately.

"Cardinal Orsini writes that the Colonna family is seeking new alliances through marriage," Clarice said without preamble. "Their second son remains unwed."

Isabella kept her expression neutral though her heart sank. "The Colonna are closely aligned with Naples, are they not? An interesting political choice for our family at this time."

"Politics be damned," Clarice hissed, dropping her courtly facade momentarily. "You are twenty-two, Isabella. Your value as a marriage piece diminishes with each passing year. Your uncle has indulged your scholarly pursuits long enough."

Before Isabella could formulate a sufficiently diplomatic response, a servant approached with a silver salver. "A message for the Magnificent One," he announced, presenting it to Lorenzo across the room.

Lorenzo broke the unmarked seal and unfolded the parchment. The blood drained from his face as he read. Without a word, he passed the note to Michelozzi, who paled in turn.

Isabella excused herself from her aunt's presence and drifted closer to the men, straining to overhear.

"It cannot be," Michelozzi was whispering. "That bloodline was extinguished. We were certain."

"Evidently not certain enough," Lorenzo replied grimly. He glanced up, noticed Isabella's proximity, and smoothed his features into a mask of calm authority. "Gentlemen, we will continue this discussion in my private study. Isabella, my dear, would you entertain our remaining guests? Ensure they understand that Cardinal Riario's departure was expected and amicable."

It was a dismissal, thinly veiled as a request. Isabella curtsied gracefully, concealing her frustration. "Of course, Uncle. I live to serve the family's interests."

As the men withdrew, Isabella caught a glimpse of the parchment still clutched in Michelozzi's hand. Though she could not read the full message, one line stood out in elegant, blood-red ink:

"The sins of the fathers shall be visited upon the sons, even unto the third and fourth generation."

That evening, as Isabella sat at her writing desk transcribing her observations of the day, her lady's maid entered with the day's correspondence. Among the sealed letters was a small package wrapped in plain linen.

"Who delivered this?" Isabella asked, turning the package over in her hands.

"It was among the items brought up from the kitchens, my lady. The porter said it arrived with the wine deliveries."

Isabella dismissed the maid and carefully unwrapped the package. Inside, nestled in a bed of black velvet, lay a small silver key of unusual design, its handle worked into the shape of a five-petaled flower. Beneath it was a scrap of parchment bearing a single line:

"Not all Medici are blind to justice. Seek the truth in the archives, daughter of Giovanni."

Isabella's breath caught. Giovanni had been her father, Lorenzo's younger brother, dead these fifteen years from a fever. Or so she had always been told. She held the key to the light, examining its intricate workmanship. This was no ordinary key—it was crafted for a specialized lock, perhaps a document chest or private cabinet.

The reference to archives could only mean the extensive Medici collection of family records, business ledgers, and private correspondence—kept under lock and guard in the palazzo's east wing. As Lorenzo's niece, she had limited access to these archives, but certainly not to all of them.

Isabella concealed the key and message in a hidden compartment of her jewelry box, her mind racing. The night seemed suddenly alive with possibilities and dangers. Outside her window, the lights of Florence twinkled like stars fallen to earth, beautiful and remote. Somewhere among those lights moved a killer with crimson feathers and, it seemed, knowledge of Medici secrets that even she was not privy to.

She would find those secrets, Isabella resolved, wherever they might lead. Because one truth she had learned early in the Medici household: knowledge was the only currency that never devalued, the only power that could not be taken by force.

Chapter 3
The First Warning

---※---

The Medici private chapel was silent save for the soft hiss of candles burning in their holders. Lorenzo knelt before the altar, his lips moving in soundless prayer, though whether he communed with God or with his own thoughts, none could say. The chapel, like everything in the Medici orbit, served dual purposes—spiritual devotion and dynastic glorification. Donatello's bronze sculptures gleamed in the candlelight, while Lippi's frescoes depicted Biblical scenes with Medici family members inserted as holy figures, a visual assertion of divine favor.

Lorenzo crossed himself and rose, his knees protesting after an hour of devotion. Age was beginning to make itself known in his joints, a reminder of mortality that no wealth could ultimately forestall.

"You spend more time here of late, brother," came a voice from the chapel entrance.

Giuliano de' Medici, Lorenzo's younger brother, leaned against the doorframe with the casual grace that had made him the darling of Florentine society. Handsome where Lorenzo was merely striking, charming where Lorenzo was calculated, Giuliano complemented his brother in ways that strengthened the family's hold on Florence's heart.

"These are times that demand divine guidance," Lorenzo replied, moving down the aisle toward his brother. "Have you spoken with the captain of the guard?"

Giuliano fell into step beside him as they left the chapel. "Della Torre has doubled the patrols around the palazzo and placed men at all the guild headquarters. No one enters the banking district without scrutiny."

Lorenzo nodded, satisfied with these precautions if not entirely reassured. "And the other matter?"

"Our friends in Rome report unusual meetings between Cardinal Riario and representatives of both Venice and Naples. Nothing conclusive, but the timing raises questions."

The brothers walked in silence through the corridor leading to Lorenzo's private study, each lost in calculation. The relationship between Florence and the Papacy had been strained since Lorenzo had blocked the Pope's nephew from obtaining certain lucrative alum mines. That the Cardinal had appeared in Florence so soon after Pazzi's murder seemed unlikely to be coincidence.

In the study, Michelozzi awaited with a stack of correspondence requiring Lorenzo's attention. The secretary dismissed himself with a bow as the brothers entered, but Lorenzo called him back.

"The message from this morning. Have you determined how it entered the palazzo?"

Michelozzi's face tightened. "No, my lord. None of the servants admit to carrying it, and the guards swear no unauthorized messenger passed their posts. It simply... appeared on the salver."

"Which means we have either a liar or a ghost in our household," Giuliano remarked, helping himself to wine from a carafe. "I find liars more plausible, generally speaking."

Lorenzo waved Michelozzi away and turned to a map of Florence spread across a table. Carved wooden markers representing major family holdings and political alliances dotted the parchment—a physical manifestation of the complex web of power Lorenzo monitored constantly.

"If this is the opening move in a new conspiracy against us," Lorenzo said, "we must identify the players quickly. The Pazzi are obvious suspects, given the victim's family connection."

"Too obvious," Giuliano countered. "If they sought revenge against us, why kill one of their own? Besides, Francesco Pazzi practically grovels at your feet these days, desperate for banking partnerships."

Lorenzo's finger traced the outline of the city walls on the map. "The Albizzi, then? They've never forgiven our family for their exile."

"Possible, but they lack the resources for a sustained campaign against us. And this murder..." Giuliano shook his head. "It feels like the beginning of something larger."

Lorenzo was silent for a moment, contemplating. Then, with sudden decision, he crossed to a cabinet secured with a heavy iron lock. From around his neck, he removed a key and opened the cabinet, revealing a collection of carefully preserved documents—the most sensitive of the Medici archives.

"There are older grudges than those held by the Albizzi," Lorenzo said quietly, removing a bound volume of yellowed parchment. "Grievances buried so deep that most believe them forgotten."

Giuliano's brow furrowed. "You think this connects to the Visconti affair? That was nearly forty years ago, in our father's time."

"Forty years is nothing to a family with a long memory." Lorenzo opened the volume to a marked page. "The message this morning quoted scripture about the sins of fathers being visited on sons unto the third and fourth generation. A biblical veneer for a very worldly vengeance."

Before Giuliano could respond, a commotion erupted in the corridor outside—raised voices, hurried footsteps, then a sharp knock at the study door.

"Enter," Lorenzo called, hastily returning the document to its cabinet.

A palace guard burst in, his face flushed. "My lords, forgive the interruption. A package has arrived for the Magnificent One. The manner of its delivery... the captain thought you should be informed immediately."

The brothers exchanged glances. "What manner of delivery?" Giuliano asked.

"It was found hanging from the neck of the lion statue at the palazzo entrance. No one saw it placed there, despite the guards." The man's voice dropped. "And there was blood, my lords. Fresh blood smeared on the statue's mane."

Lorenzo straightened. "Bring this package. But first, clear the main corridors of all visitors and non-essential personnel. And send word to Captain della Torre that I wish to see him at once."

When the guard had gone, Giuliano moved to close the study windows. "A bold provocateur, to reach the very door of the palazzo unseen."

"Bold, or desperate to be noticed," Lorenzo countered. "Either way, we shall learn more soon enough."

Within minutes, della Torre himself arrived bearing a small wooden box, roughly the size of a man's hand. The seasoned captain's face was grim as he placed it on Lorenzo's desk.

"No one has opened it, as you instructed. It bears no outward markings save for this," della Torre pointed to a small symbol burned into the lid—a stylized fleur-de-lis, but with five petals rather than the traditional three.

Lorenzo's face remained impassive, but Giuliano noticed his brother's knuckles whitening as he gripped the edge of the desk. "Leave us, Captain. Double the guard on Isabella's chambers, and ensure my wife and children are secure in the family wing. No one enters or leaves without my explicit permission."

When they were alone, Lorenzo stared at the box as if it might spring to life. "The five-petaled lily," he murmured. "So it is true."

"What is true?" Giuliano demanded. "Lorenzo, you've suspected something since the murder. What aren't you telling me?"

Instead of answering, Lorenzo retrieved a thin dagger from his desk drawer and carefully pried open the box lid. Inside, nestled on a bed of crimson silk, lay a small silver object—a thimble, tarnished with age but clearly valuable by its craftsmanship.

Beneath it was a folded piece of parchment. With steady hands that belied his inner turmoil, Lorenzo unfolded the note and read aloud:

"Blood calls to blood across the years. The debt of five lives shall be paid in full. The masked one comes for what is owed. Ave Maria, piena di grazia..."

The Latin prayer trailed off into a smear of what appeared to be dried blood. Lorenzo cursed softly under his breath, a rare lapse in his careful self-control.

"A thimble?" Giuliano asked, confused. "What significance—"

"It belonged to our grandmother," Lorenzo interrupted. "A gift from our grandfather Cosimo upon the birth of their first child. It has been missing since before our father's death."

Giuliano paled. "How could someone outside the family possess such an item? And what does this mean, 'the debt of five lives'?"

Lorenzo returned the thimble to its box with careful reverence. "There are chapters of our family history that were deemed best forgotten, brother. Decisions made in difficult times to secure the future of both the Medici and Florence itself."

"What decisions?" Giuliano's voice had taken on an edge. "What have we never been told?"

Lorenzo looked at his younger brother for a long moment, weighing decades of protective silence against present necessity.

"In 1433," he began slowly, "when our grandfather was temporarily exiled by the Albizzi faction, there was another family who stood against us—the Vinciguerra. Unlike the Albizzi, who sought political dominance, the Vinciguerra challenged our very right to exist. Their patriarch, Umberto Vinciguerra, claimed that our rise from merchants to rulers was an abomination against the natural order."

Lorenzo paced as he continued, his voice taking on the quality of a historian recounting ancient events. "When Cosimo returned from exile and solidified his power, the Vinciguerra did not submit like the other families. Instead, they conspired with mercenaries from Milan for an armed coup. Had they succeeded, Florence would have become a puppet state, and every Medici would have hanged from the Palazzo della Signoria."

"I've never heard of this family," Giuliano said. "In any chronicle or record."

"Because they were erased," Lorenzo replied bluntly. "Not just defeated, but expunged from Florence's memory. The five male heirs of the family disappeared on a single night in 1439. The official record states they fled to Venice after their plot was discovered. The truth is more... complicated."

Giuliano sank into a chair, absorbing the implication. "And this killer believes himself to be what—a Vinciguerra descendant seeking vengeance for these five men?"

"Or someone using that history to destabilize us in the present," Lorenzo said. "Either way, the threat is immediate and directed at the heart of our family."

Before Giuliano could respond, Isabella appeared in the doorway, her face flushed from hurried movement. "Uncle, the captain said you ordered me confined to my chambers. What has happened?"

Lorenzo hesitated, conscious of how much Isabella had already overheard. His niece was brilliant but untested in true crisis. Yet if this threat targeted all Medici, she deserved to know the danger.

"Come in, child, and close the door," he said finally. "There are matters of family security we must discuss."

Isabella complied, her sharp eyes taking in the wooden box, the parchment, and the tense posture of both brothers. She remained standing, back straight, every inch the Medici despite her gender.

"Another message from the killer?" she asked directly.

Lorenzo nodded, unsurprised by her intuition. "Not just messages now. A warning, delivered to our very door."

He explained the situation in broad strokes, omitting the specific details of the Vinciguerra affair but emphasizing the seriousness of the threat. As he spoke, Lorenzo watched Isabella carefully, noting how she processed the information—analytically rather than emotionally, her mind visibly working through implications and possibilities.

"So this killer believes our family committed some ancient wrong and seeks retribution," she summarized when he had finished. "But why begin with Pazzi rather than striking directly at a Medici?"

"A pertinent question," Lorenzo acknowledged. "Gian Lorenzo Pazzi was distantly related to our mother's cousin by marriage—hardly a blow to our family heart."

"Unless..." Isabella began, then hesitated.

"Speak freely," Lorenzo encouraged. "In this crisis, we need every perspective."

"Unless the murders are not the true attack, but merely signals announcing it," she suggested. "The killer takes five lives to balance the five allegedly taken by our ancestors. But what if the real vengeance lies in exposing whatever happened to the Vinciguerra family? A knife to the heart kills quickly; a secret revealed can destroy a legacy forever."

The brothers exchanged glances, struck by the insight. "From the mouths of the young," Giuliano murmured.

Lorenzo nodded slowly. "It would align with the theatrical nature of the warnings. This is someone who craves audience and acknowledgment. They kill to command attention, but their ultimate aim may indeed be revelation rather than mere bloodshed."

"Then we have two urgent tasks," Isabella said, warming to her analysis. "First, secure all records relating to this Vinciguerra affair, lest the killer obtain and distribute them. Second, identify potential targets for the remaining four murders, as these will lead us to the killer."

Lorenzo looked at his niece with newfound respect. "Sound reasoning. The archives will be moved to the secure vault beneath the old banking hall tonight. As for potential victims..." he trailed off, his mind working through possibilities.

"If Pazzi was chosen for his distant connection to our bloodline," Giuliano suggested, "then perhaps the next victims will share some characteristic with the five Vinciguerra men who disappeared."

"We need more information," Isabella said decisively. "Uncle, I could research these events in the family archives before they're moved. As a woman, I might notice connections that others overlook."

Lorenzo considered the request. Normally, he would protect Isabella from such darkness, but these were not normal times. Moreover, her intelligence and outside perspective might indeed uncover patterns invisible to those more directly involved.

"Very well," he decided. "You will work with Michelozzi tomorrow to examine the relevant documents. But you are not to share what you learn with anyone outside this room, nor are you to leave the palazzo without armed escort. Understood?"

Isabella nodded solemnly, though inwardly she exulted at being entrusted with such responsibility. The mysterious key concealed in her chamber seemed to burn in her thoughts, but she maintained her composed expression. "I understand fully, Uncle. Family above all."

"Family above all," the brothers echoed—the unofficial Medici motto, spoken in moments requiring absolute loyalty.

As the meeting concluded and Isabella prepared to return to her chambers, Lorenzo caught her arm gently. "One more thing, child. If you should come across any reference to a five-petaled lily or a masquerade mask in your research, bring it directly to me. Regardless of context."

Isabella promised she would, filing away this curious instruction alongside her growing collection of mysteries. As she walked the dimly lit corridor back to her chambers, flanked by guards her uncle had assigned, she felt the weight of unspoken histories pressing down like the vaulted ceilings above. The Medici palazzo, once merely her home, now seemed full of shadows and secrets waiting to be uncovered.

And somewhere in Florence, a killer was planning the next act in a drama generations in the making—a production where every Medici had been cast in a role they never chose to play.

Chapter 4
The Masked Killer Strikes Again

The body of Tommaso Altoviti was discovered shortly after dawn in the courtyard of his own palazzo. Unlike the frenzied scene that had surrounded Pazzi's murder, this discovery was marked by an eerie silence. The servants had found their master seated at his desk in the loggia overlooking the garden, slumped forward as if in sleep. Only when they approached to wake him did they realize that sleep had nothing to do with his stillness.

By the time Captain della Torre arrived, the household was in carefully controlled chaos. Altoviti's widow, a formidable woman from the Strozzi family, had ordered the body untouched and the gates locked. No one had entered or left since the discovery.

"He sits as if still working," she told della Torre, her voice steady despite the circumstances. "Were it not for the blood, one might think him merely exhausted from his labors."

The captain approached the body cautiously. Altoviti had been Florence's most prominent moneylender, known for extracting exorbitant interest from desperate borrowers. His practices had made him wealthy and despised in equal measure. Now he sat at his desk, a quill still clutched in his right hand, ledgers open before him. The only indication of violence was a thin line of blood that had trickled from his ears, nose, and the corners of his eyes, staining the parchment beneath.

"No visible wounds," della Torre murmured, circling the body. Then he noticed something peculiar: a small puncture mark at the base of the skull, almost hidden by the collar of Altoviti's rich brocade robe. "Except here. Someone drove a thin blade into his brainstem."

"A quick death, then?" asked Lorenzo de' Medici, who had arrived moments earlier with his personal physician in tow.

"Painless, even," the physician confirmed after a brief examination. "A technique used by some battlefield surgeons to end the suffering of mortally wounded soldiers. It requires intimate knowledge of anatomy."

Lorenzo's face hardened into the mask of calculation that had earned him Florence's fear as well as its admiration. "Then they are to intervene with whatever force is necessary. But I want this villain alive, Captain. Dead men tell no tales, and we need to know who else might be involved in this conspiracy."

As della Torre departed to arrange the surveillance, Lorenzo remained alone in the council chamber. He moved to the narrow window overlooking the Piazza della Signoria below, where Florentines went about their daily business, blissfully unaware of the shadow hanging over their city's most powerful family.

His fingers traced the outline of the burned parchment fragment in his sleeve. Some secrets, he reflected grimly, were buried so deep that even he—heir to the Medici legacy—knew them only in fragments and whispers. What had his grandfather done on that October night in 1439? What "necessary measures" had been authorized against these mysterious five? And most troubling of all: how had knowledge of these events survived to haunt a new generation?

Behind the desk, partially hidden by Altoviti's slumped form, della Torre discovered what he had been dreading—another crimson feather, this one pierced through with a golden pin into the fine leather of the chair.

"He leaves his signature again," Lorenzo observed, his voice tight. "A performer who craves acknowledgment."

The captain carefully removed the feather, noticing something he had missed at first glance. "There is writing on this one." He held it to the light, squinting at the minuscule script that ran along the quill. "Latin... 'Avaritia'."

"Greed," Lorenzo translated immediately. "A judgment, then. Altoviti was known for his usurious rates."

As they examined the scene further, della Torre's lieutenant called from the adjacent chamber. "Captain! You must see this."

The adjoining room had been Altoviti's private meditation space, a fashionable affectation among Florence's elite who wished to appear spiritually contemplative despite their worldly pursuits. Now it had been transformed into something altogether more disturbing.

The walls, previously adorned with devotional paintings, had been draped in crimson silk. Candles had been arranged in a perfect pentagon on the floor, all burned down to stubs. But what commanded immediate attention was the object suspended from the ceiling—a mask, hanging by silken threads.

Not the colorful, festive disguise of Carnival, but something far more disquieting. It was crafted of porcelain-white leather, its features refined yet subtly inhuman. The eyes were almond-shaped hollows, elongated and angled upward like those of a predatory bird. The mouth was a thin, straight line incised into the material, giving no hint of expression. Most disturbing were the tears—five of them—rendered in gold leaf trailing down from each eye socket.

"Beautifully made," Lorenzo murmured, his art patron's eye unwillingly appreciating the craftsmanship. "The work of a master leatherworker."

"But not worn," della Torre noted. "This is not the killer's actual mask—it's a message."

Lorenzo approached cautiously, studying the suspended object. "A theater mask. The ancients used such faces to portray fixed characters—the grieving widow, the jealous husband, the avenging spirit."

"Which character does this represent?" the captain asked.

"Justice," came a voice from the doorway. Isabella stood there, flanked by impatient guards who had clearly failed to prevent her entry. "Though not the justice of courts and magistrates. The justice of blood debts and ancestral oaths."

Lorenzo frowned at his niece's presence but did not dismiss her. "How would you know such a thing?"

Isabella stepped into the room, careful not to disturb any potential evidence. "Last night I began the research you requested. I found references to a theater troupe patronized by the Vinciguerra family before their... disappearance. They specialized in ancient Greek tragedies involving familial retribution." She pointed to the mask. "Their emblem was the face of Nemesis, the goddess of divine vengeance."

Lorenzo's expression darkened. "You've been busy, niece. What else did your research uncover?"

"That five masks were commissioned by Umberto Vinciguerra just weeks before the family vanished. Each represented a different aspect of justice—divine, earthly, poetic, military, and..." she hesitated, "familial. Together, they were called 'The Faces of Retribution.'"

Della Torre circled the mask, careful not to touch it. "If this is one of those original masks, it would be over forty years old. Yet it appears newly made."

30

"A recreation," Lorenzo concluded. "Someone with knowledge of the original design has crafted a new set. The question is: how many of the five have been completed, and how many murders do they portend?"

Isabella moved closer to her uncle. "The archives mentioned that each mask corresponded to a specific method of execution. This one—" she gestured to the hanging face with its golden tears, "—signifies poison or disease. Yet Altoviti was killed with a blade."

"A discrepancy," Lorenzo mused. "Or perhaps our killer adapts the methods to practical necessity."

Della Torre's attention had shifted to something beneath the hanging mask—a small wooden chest, ornately carved with intertwining lilies. The five-petaled variation appeared prominently on its lid.

"My lord," he called, kneeling beside the object. "Another message awaits."

Lorenzo joined him, examining the chest without touching it. "No lock."

"Shall I open it?" the captain asked, hand hovering over the lid.

Lorenzo hesitated, then nodded. "Carefully."

Della Torre lifted the lid to reveal a collection of items arranged with deliberate precision: a set of banking ledgers bound with red ribbon, a silver florin bearing Cosimo de' Medici's profile, a small vial of dark liquid, and a folded piece of parchment sealed with black wax. The seal bore no family crest, only the imprint of a stylized mask similar to the one hanging above.

Lorenzo broke the seal and unfolded the parchment. As he read, the blood drained from his face. Without a word, he handed it to della Torre, who read aloud:

"The usurer who drinks the blood of desperate men has paid his debt. Four remain to balance the scales. When the pentagon is complete, the truth shall wear five faces, and Florence will know the name of Vinciguerra once more. The Magnificent One is invited to stop this judgment—he need only confess the crimes of his blood and return what was stolen. Ave Maria, piena di grazia..."

Again, the prayer ended in a smear of brownish-red.

"Blood," Isabella whispered. "But whose?"

Lorenzo's face had settled into a mask of grim determination. "Captain, I want every banker, moneylender, and financial official with connections to my family under guard immediately. If this killer follows the pattern I suspect, the remaining victims will all share some characteristic with the Vinciguerra five."

"And what characteristic is that, my lord?" della Torre asked.

"Power brokers who rose from humble origins," Lorenzo replied after a moment's calculation. "Men whose influence exceeds their bloodline. The Vinciguerra despised such ascension—they believed power should remain with ancient noble houses, not merchants and craftsmen like my grandfather."

Isabella's quick mind made the connection. "They would have included your family in this judgment. The Medici were wool merchants before becoming bankers."

"Precisely," Lorenzo nodded. "This vendetta is against not just our family, but what we represent—Florence's meritocracy, where talent and industry can elevate a house beyond its origins."

Della Torre had been examining the vial from the chest. "My lord, this appears to be poison. Should we assume the killer planned to use this on Altoviti but changed his method?"

"Or it's intended for a future victim," Isabella suggested. "These displays seem meticulously planned—nothing would be left without purpose."

Lorenzo took the vial carefully, studying its contents. "Have your physician examine this, Captain. Knowing the compound might help identify where it was procured." His gaze returned to the hanging mask, its hollow eyes seeming to follow his movements. "In the meantime, I want this evidence removed to the palazzo. The fewer who see these... theatrical arrangements, the better."

As officers began carefully documenting and collecting the items, Lorenzo drew Isabella aside. "Your presence here was not requested, niece. The palazzo was to be secured."

Isabella met his gaze steadily. "The guards were distracted by a commotion in the kitchens—something about spoiled wine. I took the opportunity to follow you because I believed my research might prove relevant." A pause. "It seems I was correct."

Lorenzo studied her face, recognizing the determined intelligence that mirrored his own. "You were. But such initiative carries risk. This killer has demonstrated an ability to penetrate secure locations unseen. No Medici is safe."

"All the more reason to pool our resources," Isabella countered. "Uncle, I can access spaces and conversations closed to you and your men. Let me help hunt this phantom."

Before Lorenzo could respond, a commotion erupted from the courtyard below. Moments later, Giuliano burst into the room, his handsome face flushed with exertion.

"Brother," he addressed Lorenzo without preamble, "another body has been found."

Lorenzo stiffened. "Where? Who?"

"Cardinal Orsini's secretary, Stefano Bardi. His throat was cut in the garden of Santa Croce monastery."

"The papal connection," Lorenzo murmured. "This complicates matters."

"There's more," Giuliano continued grimly. "A message was carved into his chest: 'Ask the Magnificent what became of the girl.' And this was left clutched in his hand." He held out a small object—a child's wooden doll, its face blackened as if burned.

Isabella watched her uncle's reaction carefully, noting how his composed expression faltered momentarily, a flash of genuine fear crossing his features before being quickly suppressed.

"Captain," Lorenzo turned to della Torre, his voice now iron-hard, "return to the palazzo immediately. Double the guard on the family wing, and bring Michelozzi to my study. No one enters or leaves without verification by at least two known loyalists."

Della Torre bowed and departed swiftly, barking orders to his men.

"Giuliano, secure the Signoria. The Priors must be warned that this is escalating from murder to potential insurrection. Frame it as a threat to civic stability, not merely a Medici concern."

As Giuliano nodded and turned to leave, Lorenzo grasped Isabella's arm. "You will return to the palazzo with me. Your research must continue, but under stricter supervision."

"The girl," Isabella said quietly. "What girl, Uncle?"

Lorenzo's eyes darkened. "A matter from before your birth. Nothing that concerns present dangers."

But Isabella had caught the lie in his averted gaze. Whatever—or whoever—the message referred to had struck Lorenzo more deeply than the deaths themselves.

As they departed Altoviti's palazzo, Lorenzo moved with the calculated precision of a man accustomed to crisis. Yet Isabella noticed his eyes darting to shadows, scanning rooftops and windows with newfound wariness. The Magnificent One, ruler of Florence in all but name, had begun to fear the darkness.

In the carriage returning them to the Medici palace, Isabella watched Florence pass by through narrow windows. The city seemed unchanged—merchants hawking wares, scholars debating in piazzas, artisans bent over their work. Yet now she saw it through different eyes, aware that somewhere among these familiar streets moved a killer with a meticulous plan and intimate knowledge of secrets buried for decades.

The sun was setting, casting long shadows across the Arno River. As darkness fell, Isabella could not help but wonder where the masked figure would strike next—and who among them would survive to see the dawn.

Chapter 5
The Investigation Begins

Dawn broke over Florence, painting the terracotta rooftops with golden light that belied the darkness gathering within the city's walls. In the map room of the Medici palazzo, Lorenzo stood surrounded by his most trusted advisors, the atmosphere heavy with tension. Before them lay a large table upon which Captain della Torre had arranged the evidence from both murders: sketches of the wounds, the crimson feathers, and meticulous drawings of the mask found at Altoviti's residence.

"Two murders in as many days," Lorenzo said, his voice tight with controlled anger. "Both with clear connections to our family, both executed with theatrical precision."

Michelozzi, who had aged visibly since the discovery of the first body, spread out a parchment bearing a hastily drawn diagram. "We've mapped the locations of both killings. Pazzi was found here, near the eastern gate. Altoviti in his own home, here in the banking district. Bardi at Santa Croce, directly east of the Signoria."

"A pattern?" Giuliano asked, leaning forward to study the markings.

"Perhaps," the secretary replied. "If we connect these points..." His quill traced lines between the murder sites, forming a partial geometric shape.

"A pentagon," Isabella murmured, earning sharp glances from the men. "The killer referenced it in his message: 'When the pentagon is complete.' Five points, five victims."

Lorenzo nodded grimly. "Five for the five Vinciguerra heirs." He turned to della Torre. "What of the strange markings reported on the bodies?"

The captain produced another parchment. "Pazzi bore five puncture wounds arranged in this pattern." He indicated a star-like formation on the diagram. "Altoviti had nothing visible save the entry wound at his skull, but upon closer examination by your physician, we discovered this burned into the skin beneath his clothing." The drawing showed a complex symbol resembling a stylized eye encircled by flames.

"And Bardi?" Lorenzo prompted.

"Beyond the message carved into his chest, a similar mark was found on his inner wrist." Della Torre pointed to another symbol, this one appearing like intertwined serpents forming a knot. "Each differs, yet they share common elements."

Poliziano, the humanist scholar, had been silent until now. "They are alchemical symbols," he said suddenly. "Modified, but recognizable to those versed in the hermetic arts. This one," he pointed to the eye, "represents purification through fire. And this," indicating the serpent knot, "transformation of base matter to divine essence."

"Alchemy?" Giuliano scoffed. "What has that mystical nonsense to do with murder?"

"More than you might imagine," Poliziano replied evenly. "Many noble families—including the Vinciguerra—were patrons of alchemical research. Not for gold-making, but for the philosophical principles that underpinned the practice. The transformation of the impure to the pure, the earthly to the divine."

"Or the common to the noble," Isabella suggested. "Uncle, you said the Vinciguerra believed power should rest only with ancient bloodlines. Perhaps these symbols represent their belief in the natural hierarchy—a hierarchy our family violated by rising from merchants to rulers."

Lorenzo's mouth tightened with grudging approval. "A plausible connection. But symbols and theatrics tell us nothing of practical value. We need the killer's identity, not his philosophical justifications."

Della Torre cleared his throat. "There is one peculiarity that may narrow our search. The blade used on Pazzi was extremely specialized—a triangular stiletto of unusual length. Few armorers in Florence craft such weapons."

"Begin there," Lorenzo ordered. "Visit every swordsmith and armorer in the city. Find who commissioned or purchased such a blade."

As the council continued to debate strategy, Isabella's attention drifted to a curious absence in the evidence before them. "The doll," she said suddenly. "The burned doll found with Bardi. Where is it?"

A heavy silence fell over the room. Lorenzo and Michelozzi exchanged a look that Isabella couldn't interpret.

"It is being examined separately," Lorenzo said smoothly—too smoothly. "Captain, continue your report."

But Isabella had caught something in her uncle's manner that raised her suspicions. The doll had affected him deeply, yet now he sought to divert attention from it. Another piece to the puzzle, another secret withheld.

Later that morning, Isabella stood in the Medici archives, a vast chamber beneath the palazzo where the family's records were stored. Normally, access was strictly controlled, but Lorenzo had authorized her research—albeit under Michelozzi's watchful eye. The elderly secretary hovered nearby as she carefully examined ledgers dating back to Cosimo's time.

"What exactly are we seeking?" Michelozzi asked, his voice echoing in the cavernous space.

Isabella turned a brittle page, scanning columns of numbers and names. "Connections between our family and the Vinciguerra before their disappearance. Financial dealings, political alliances, anything that might illuminate their relationship."

"You won't find much," Michelozzi said. "After their... departure, most records concerning them were removed from public chronicles."

"But not from our private archives," Isabella countered. "The Medici forget nothing, especially where money is concerned."

Hours passed as they worked in silence, dust motes dancing in the shafts of light that penetrated the underground chamber through narrow windows near the ceiling. Isabella's eyes burned from strain, but her determination never wavered.

Near midday, she discovered something curious—a series of payments recorded in a ledger from 1438, made to a name she didn't recognize: Maestro Silvestro Carvaggio.

"Who was this Carvaggio?" she asked Michelozzi. "The sums are substantial."

The old man squinted at the entry. "Ah, him. A craftsman of some renown. Specialized in theatrical masks and props for the mystery plays performed at Easter and Christmas."

"The same plays the Vinciguerra patronized," Isabella noted, remembering her earlier research. "Five large payments in the months before their disappearance. Could Cosimo have commissioned the same artisan who created the original masks?"

Michelozzi's expression grew guarded. "What a strange coincidence that would be."

"Is there any record of this Carvaggio after 1439?"

"I believe he relocated to Venice shortly after... certain events occurred."

Isabella's mind raced with possibilities. "A master craftsman skilled in creating masks, removed from Florence just after the Vinciguerra vanished. Perhaps to eliminate a witness?"

Michelozzi looked distinctly uncomfortable. "Speculation without evidence is dangerous, Lady Isabella."

"Then let us find evidence," she replied firmly. "Were any of Carvaggio's works preserved in our collections? Sketches, designs, anything?"

The secretary hesitated. "There might be something in the east vault. Your grandfather was meticulous about preserving artifacts of historical significance."

Isabella was already moving toward the indicated section, her excitement mounting. The east vault was a smaller chamber, secured with an iron-bound door that Michelozzi unlocked with a key from his belt. Inside, wooden cabinets lined the walls, each containing drawers and shelves filled with documents and objects deemed too sensitive or valuable for the main archives.

"Third cabinet from the right," Michelozzi directed reluctantly. "Bottom drawer."

The drawer slid open with a protesting groan, revealing a leather portfolio tied with faded ribbon. Isabella untied it with careful fingers and spread its contents across a nearby table. Inside were sketches and designs for theatrical masks—dozens of them, rendered in exquisite detail.

"These are magnificent," she breathed, examining the artistry. The masks depicted various historical and mythological figures, each bearing the signature flourish of detailed work around the eyes.

At the bottom of the portfolio, a separate packet wrapped in silk caught her attention. She unwrapped it to reveal five detailed design sketches, each more disturbing than the last. Unlike the other masks, which were celebratory or dramatic, these exuded menace. They shared the same basic shape but differed in their details: one wept golden tears, another featured a mouth twisted in rage, a third bore the visage of calculated coldness.

"The Faces of Retribution," Isabella whispered, recognizing what she had found. "The original designs commissioned by the Vinciguerra."

Michelozzi had gone pale. "Lady Isabella, I don't think—"

"But this makes no sense," she continued, ignoring his discomfort. "Why would Cosimo preserve designs commissioned by his enemies? Unless..." Her voice trailed off as she noticed something curious about the sketches. In the corner of each was a small notation: measurements and a name.

"These weren't just designs," she realized with growing horror. "They were fitted to specific individuals. See these notations? Each mask was created for one of the five Vinciguerra heirs, measured to their exact features."

Michelozzi was now visibly distressed. "My lady, we should return these to storage. Your uncle would not approve—"

"What happened to them, Michelozzi?" Isabella demanded, turning to face the secretary. "What really happened to the Vinciguerra five?"

Before he could answer, a shadow fell across the table. Lorenzo stood in the doorway, his expression unreadable. "That's enough research for today, Isabella."

"Uncle," she began, gesturing to the sketches. "These masks—"

"Are part of a history best left undisturbed," Lorenzo interrupted firmly. "Michelozzi, secure these items and rejoin us in my study. Isabella, come with me."

As they walked through the dim corridors of the archives, Isabella studied her uncle's profile. "The doll," she said quietly. "It's connected to this, isn't it? 'Ask the Magnificent what became of the girl.' Who was she, Uncle?"

Lorenzo stopped abruptly, glancing around to ensure they were alone. When he spoke, his voice was barely audible. "Vinciguerra's youngest daughter. Lucia. She was eight years old when her brothers and father were... dealt with."

Isabella felt cold dread spreading through her veins. "What happened to her?"

"Officially, she perished from fever shortly after her family's exile." Lorenzo's eyes looked past Isabella, focusing on some distant memory. "The truth is more complicated."

"She survived," Isabella guessed. "You—or Grandfather—spared her."

"Cosimo was many things, but not a murderer of children," Lorenzo said sharply. "She was placed with a loyal family, given a new name and identity. She grew up never knowing her true parentage."

"Until now," Isabella whispered. "Someone has discovered her survival. Perhaps she herself has finally learned the truth."

Lorenzo's face had regained its mask-like control. "This is why the matter must be handled delicately. If a Vinciguerra heir lives, if she has children of her own who now seek vengeance..."

A commotion from the main corridors interrupted them—raised voices, hurried footsteps. A moment later, Giuliano appeared, his face flushed.

"Brother, the killer has struck again," he announced grimly. "Giovanni Tornabuoni—our own cousin—found dead in his counting house. And this time, there was a witness."

The countinghouse of the Tornabuoni bank stood in the heart of Florence's financial district, a stone's throw from the Medici's own headquarters. By the time Lorenzo arrived with Isabella and Giuliano, della Torre had already secured the scene. The body had been discovered by a clerk arriving for the afternoon ledger review—Tornabuoni slumped at his desk, a thin blade protruding from his eye socket.

Unlike the previous victims, Giovanni had not died peacefully. The chamber bore evidence of a violent struggle: overturned furniture, scattered documents, and most tellingly, blood spattered in an arc across one wall.

"He fought back," della Torre explained, leading Lorenzo to the body. "And managed to injure his attacker. We found blood that doesn't match the victim's leading from this room to a window overlooking the side alley."

"The witness?" Lorenzo asked.

"A wine merchant making deliveries in the alley. He saw a figure climbing down from the window—cloaked in brown, with something bright crimson underneath. Most importantly, he described a mask." Della Torre's voice dropped. "White leather, with features like a bird of prey. The eyes elongated, the mouth a straight line."

Isabella exchanged glances with Lorenzo. The description matched the mask found at Altoviti's murder scene perfectly.

"Did the witness see where this figure went?" Giuliano asked.

"North, toward the cathedral. We've men searching that area now, but with the crowds..." Della Torre spread his hands in a gesture of futility.

Lorenzo approached his cousin's body, grief momentarily breaking through his composed exterior. Giovanni Tornabuoni had been more than a business associate; he had been a childhood friend, a trusted ally throughout Lorenzo's rise to power.

"Was there a message?" Lorenzo asked, steeling himself.

Della Torre produced a folded parchment. "Left on his chest. And this was driven into his hand." He held up another crimson feather, this one stained with blood at its tip.

Lorenzo read the message silently, his face darkening with each line. When he finished, he handed it to Giuliano without comment.

"'The false cousin pays the debt of betrayal,'" Giuliano read aloud. "'Three have answered. Two remain. The scales balance with blood, as they did on the night of masks. Does the Magnificent remember? Does he dream of children screaming? The girl remembers. The girl dreams. Ave Maria, piena di grazia...'"

Isabella studied the ornate script. "The handwriting matches the previous notes. But this one feels more... personal."

"And more explicit," Giuliano added grimly. "The night of masks. Children screaming. This killer wants us to know they're aware of what actually happened to the Vinciguerra."

Lorenzo had moved to examine the body, his movements methodical despite his evident distress. "Something is missing," he murmured.

"Missing?" Della Torre asked.

"Giovanni always wore a medallion—gold, bearing the Tornabuoni crest. It's gone." Lorenzo gently turned the body's head to reveal the snapped chain at the neck. "Taken as a trophy, perhaps."

Isabella had noticed something else—a symbol burned into the wood of the desk beside Tornabuoni's hand, partially hidden by scattered papers. She carefully brushed them aside to reveal an intricate design: a pentagram containing a stylized lily with five petals.

"Another alchemical symbol," she noted. "But this one seems specific to our family."

"Not to our family," Lorenzo corrected quietly. "To my grandfather." He traced the outline of the symbol with his finger. "This was Cosimo's private mark, used on his most confidential communications. Few outside the family would recognize it."

"So our killer has access to family documents," Giuliano concluded. "That narrows the field considerably."

Lorenzo straightened, his decision made. "Captain, I want the city gates closed immediately. No one enters or leaves Florence without thorough examination. Post guards at every noble residence and banking house connected to our family. The killer is injured—search every physician, barber, and apothecary who might treat such wounds."

As della Torre hurried to implement these orders, Lorenzo turned to his brother and niece. "This ends now. No more waiting for the killer to strike. We hunt them before they can claim their next victim."

"And the final target?" Giuliano asked. "Who might that be?"

Lorenzo's expression was grim. "If the pattern holds, someone close to our innermost circle. Someone whose death would strike at the heart of our family." He glanced at Isabella. "No one travels alone, not even within the palazzo. We trust no one outside this room."

As they prepared to leave, Isabella paused beside her uncle. "The night of masks," she said quietly. "What happened to the Vinciguerra five, Uncle? What did Cosimo do that now returns to haunt us?"

Lorenzo looked at her for a long moment, weighing decades of secrecy against present necessity. "Not here," he finally replied. "Tonight, when we're secure in the palazzo. You've earned the right to know—but knowledge brings its own burden, Isabella. Once told, these things cannot be unknown."

Isabella nodded solemnly. "I understand. But if we're to fight this shadow, we must first see it clearly."

As they departed the counting house, the afternoon sun was fading, casting long shadows across Florence. In the dimming light, every passerby seemed suddenly suspect, every face a potential mask hiding deadly intent. The hunt had begun—but whether they were the hunters or the hunted remained to be seen.

Chapter 6
The Medici Ball

Night had fallen over Florence, and with it came a transformation of the Medici palazzo. Despite the murders—or perhaps in defiant response to them—Lorenzo had refused to cancel the masquerade ball planned months earlier to honor visiting dignitaries from Milan and Venice. "To show fear is to invite attack," he had declared to his advisors. "Florence must see that the Medici remain unbowed."

The great hall blazed with hundreds of candles, their light reflecting off gilt decorations and jewels adorning the city's elite. Musicians played from a raised gallery, their melodies drifting over the masked revelers who spun and twirled across the marble floor. From the outside, it appeared a scene of normal magnificence—the powerful of Florence celebrating their station as they had for generations.

But beneath the veneer of festivity, tension hummed like a taut bowstring. Armed guards stood at every entrance, checking each guest thoroughly despite their rank. Lorenzo himself had positioned loyal men throughout the crowd, their masks concealing watchful eyes trained for any sign of the killer.

In her chambers, Isabella prepared for the ball with uncharacteristic attention to her appearance. Her gown of midnight blue velvet was more severe than fashionable, cut to allow freedom of movement rather than to display her figure to advantage. Beneath its voluminous folds, a small dagger in a thigh sheath provided reassurance. If the killer sought to strike at the heart of the Medici gathering, she would not be defenseless.

Her mask—silver filigree shaped like butterfly wings—concealed the upper half of her face while leaving her mouth and jaw exposed. It had been carefully chosen to allow peripheral vision and quick removal if necessary.

"You look formidable rather than fetching," observed Clarice Orsini, who had entered without knocking. Lorenzo's wife studied her niece with calculating eyes. "An unusual choice for a young woman seeking marriage prospects."

"Marriage seems a distant concern when murderers stalk our family," Isabella replied coolly.

Clarice moved further into the room, her own preparation for the ball complete. Unlike Isabella, she had opted for full Florentine opulence—crimson brocade embroidered with gold thread, pearls woven through her elaborate coiffure. Her mask, already in hand, featured the Medici and Orsini crests intertwined.

"Your uncle tells me you've been assisting with his investigation," Clarice said, her tone making clear her disapproval. "A dangerous game for a woman of your position."

"Knowledge is only dangerous to those who fear it," Isabella countered, securing her mask with silver pins.

Clarice's eyes narrowed. "You sound like your father. He too believed that truth should trump prudence." She adjusted a fold of Isabella's gown with unnecessary force. "It led him to an early grave."

Isabella stiffened. "My father died of fever."

"Is that what Lorenzo told you?" Clarice's laugh was brittle. "How convenient that the Medici control not only Florence's wealth, but its very history."

Before Isabella could demand clarification, trumpet fanfare announced the formal beginning of the ball. Clarice's secrets would have to wait.

"Remember your station tonight," the older woman advised as they prepared to descend. "You represent our family to all of

Florence. Whatever... investigative urges you feel should be suppressed in favor of appropriate behavior."

Isabella smiled thinly. "I'll comport myself with the dignity expected of a Medici woman, Aunt. You need not concern yourself."

The grand staircase offered a perfect view of the assembled guests below—a sea of masked faces turned upward in anticipation as Lorenzo and Giuliano took their positions at the center of the hall. The brothers made a striking pair: Lorenzo in deep crimson velvet, his mask a simple black domino that emphasized rather than concealed his distinctively hooded eyes; Giuliano resplendent in azure trimmed with silver, his golden hair gleaming above a mask depicting Apollo, god of light and reason.

Isabella and Clarice joined them at the foot of the stairs, completing the family tableau. As they moved through the crowd, accepting greetings and homage, Isabella maintained a watchful awareness of their surroundings. Della Torre had positioned his men strategically throughout the room, but in this sea of masks, the killer could hide in plain sight.

"Your presence reassures the city," Cardinal Riario murmured to Lorenzo as the family passed his position. "Though some might consider a celebration imprudent given recent... unpleasantness."

"Florence does not cower before shadows," Lorenzo replied smoothly. "Nor do the Medici."

The Cardinal's thin smile never reached his eyes. "Courage and folly often wear similar masks, Magnifico. One wonders if you can distinguish between them."

As diplomatic barbs continued to fly beneath the veneer of courteous conversation, Isabella circulated through the hall, scanning the crowd for anything unusual. The city's most powerful families were all represented—the Pazzi, the Strozzi, the Albizzi—each watching the others with the calculation of chess players contemplating their next moves.

Near the western colonnade, Isabella noticed a figure who seemed out of place among the wealthy merchants and nobles. A man of average height, dressed in fine but understated brown velvet, wearing a mask of unusual design—not the colorful creations favored by the Florentine elite, but something simpler and more elegant. A half-mask of pale leather covered only the upper portion of his face, its surface unadorned save for subtle tooling around the eyes that created the impression of constant vigilance.

As if sensing her scrutiny, the man turned. Their gazes met across the crowded hall, and Isabella felt a peculiar shock of recognition, though she was certain they had never met. There was something in his bearing, in the controlled precision of his movements, that seemed familiar.

The stranger inclined his head in acknowledgment before melting into the crowd. Without conscious decision, Isabella found herself following, drawn by instinct and curiosity. She moved carefully through the press of bodies, maintaining visual contact with his brown-clad back as he navigated toward the less crowded gallery overlooking the gardens.

Outside, the night air provided welcome relief from the stuffy heat of the ballroom. Torches illuminated the formal gardens, where some guests had escaped to stroll the paths or engage in more private conversations. Isabella hesitated at the threshold, scanning the shadows for her quarry.

"Lady Isabella de' Medici," came a voice from her left. "Your pursuit was admirably subtle, though unnecessary. I would have sought you out eventually."

She turned to find the stranger leaning against a marble balustrade, his mask now removed to reveal a face of arresting intensity. Not conventionally handsome, but striking—high cheekbones, a straight nose, and eyes of such dark brown they appeared almost black in the torchlight. His age was difficult to determine—perhaps thirty, perhaps older—but he carried himself with the confidence of experience.

"You have the advantage of me, sir," Isabella replied carefully, maintaining a safe distance. "You know my name, but I don't know yours."

The man smiled slightly. "Names have power, my lady. They open doors and close others. For now, let us say I am a student of Florence's true history—not the sanitized version commemorated in statues and frescoes."

Isabella's hand drifted closer to where her dagger was concealed. "A historian, then?"

"Of sorts." He gestured to the mask in his hand. "Though some might call me a collector. Specifically, of objects that others wish forgotten."

A chill that had nothing to do with the night air spread through Isabella's veins. "Objects such as Venetian masks? Or perhaps crimson feathers?"

The stranger's expression remained impassive, but something flickered in his eyes—approval, perhaps. "You are as perceptive as they say. Your uncle's blood shows strongly in you, though I suspect you've inherited more than just his intellect."

"Who are you?" Isabella demanded, abandoning pretense. "What connection do you have to these murders?"

"A complicated question with many answers." He straightened, moving a step closer. "Perhaps the better question is: what do you know of the Vinciguerra family and their fate?"

Isabella tensed, prepared to call for the guards. "Enough to understand the motive behind these killings. Revenge for ancient wrongs."

The stranger's smile deepened, revealing unexpected warmth. "Not revenge, Lady Isabella. Justice. The distinction is important."

"Justice does not come from murder," she countered.

"Doesn't it? Ask your uncle what justice was served that October night in 1439." He reached slowly into his doublet, withdrawing a small object that gleamed in the torchlight—a golden medallion on a broken chain. "This belonged to Giovanni Tornabuoni. Do you know why I took it?"

Isabella felt ice form in her stomach. "You. You're the killer."

The man made a dismissive gesture. "A crude label for a complex role. I am an instrument, nothing more."

"An instrument of what?"

"Restoration." He held the medallion up, letting it catch the light. "Did you know that this was once Vinciguerra property? Stolen along with five lives and a family legacy. I merely return it to its rightful circulation." He tossed it suddenly, and Isabella caught it reflexively.

"A gift," he said, "and a warning. Three have paid the debt. Two remain. Unless your uncle acknowledges the truth and makes amends."

Isabella clutched the medallion, its metal warm against her palm. "What truth? What amends could possibly justify murder?"

The stranger's expression hardened. "Ask Lorenzo about the masks. Ask him what sounds they made when placed on living faces. Ask him about the girl who witnessed it all."

From inside the palazzo, music swelled as a new dance began. The man glanced toward the doors, then back to Isabella. "Our time grows short. Remember this: not all that the Medici buried has remained in the ground. Some truths claw their way back to the surface, no matter how deep they're interred."

Before Isabella could respond, he stepped backward into deeper shadow. "Until our next meeting, Lady Isabella. I look forward to seeing which path you choose when you learn what legacy your family has truly bestowed upon you."

With that, he was gone, slipping into the darkness of the garden with unsettling grace. Isabella stood frozen, the medallion clutched in her hand, mind racing with implications and questions. The killer had walked among them, had spoken directly to her—not with madness or hatred, but with the measured conviction of someone who believed absolutely in the righteousness of his cause.

More disturbing still was the sense that he had told her the truth, at least as he perceived it. What had happened on that October night so long ago? What had her grandfather done that now returned to haunt the next generation?

The medallion grew heavy in her hand. A trophy from his latest victim, yes—but also a message meant specifically for her. Why her? What role did he envision for the niece of his primary target?

Inside, the music continued, oblivious to the deadly game being played within the palazzo walls. Isabella took a deep breath, composing herself before returning to the ball. She would find Lorenzo, show him the medallion, tell him of this encounter. Together they would unravel this conspiracy before more blood stained the Medici name.

But as she turned toward the doors, a sudden thought stopped her. The stranger had known where to find her, had anticipated her movements with uncanny precision. How had he gained such intimate knowledge of the palazzo and its occupants? The answer was as obvious as it was disturbing: he had help from within.

Someone close to the Medici was collaborating with the killer—feeding him information, granting him access, perhaps even assisting in the murders themselves. Isabella scanned the glittering crowd through the open doors. Behind every mask might hide the face of betrayal.

Trust no one outside this room, Lorenzo had said. But now Isabella wondered if even that small circle of trust was too wide.

The hunt had indeed begun, but the prey and predator were no longer clearly defined. As Isabella slipped the medallion into her bodice and composed her features into a mask of calm, she realized that the greatest performance of the evening was not on the dance floor, but in the deadly game of secrets and lies playing out beneath the surface of Medici power.

And somewhere in Florence, the remaining two masks waited to be worn, their empty eye sockets seeming to watch with patient, eternal hunger for the blood that would complete their pentagon of vengeance.

Chapter 7
The Family Crypt

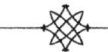

Morning found Isabella in the Medici family chapel, kneeling before the elaborate tomb of Cosimo de' Medici. She had not slept after the masquerade, her mind too consumed with the stranger's words and the weight of Tornabuoni's medallion, now hidden in her chamber. The chapel was silent save for the whisper of her own breathing and the occasional scurry of a mouse behind the ornate wall panels.

"Seeking ancestral guidance?" Lorenzo's voice broke the stillness as he entered the chapel alone. In the pale light filtering through stained glass, he looked haggard, the toll of recent days evident in the new lines etched around his eyes.

Isabella rose, smoothing her skirts. "Seeking answers. Did della Torre find any trace of our uninvited guest from last night?"

"None." Lorenzo's mouth tightened. "He vanished like morning mist. The guards swear no stranger left through any gate, which means either incompetence or complicity."

"Or perhaps our killer knows passages through this city that even you don't," Isabella suggested.

Lorenzo studied his niece carefully. "You seem remarkably composed for someone who conversed with a murderer."

"I've had time to consider his words." Isabella moved closer to Cosimo's tomb, trailing her fingers along the cool marble. "He spoke of justice, not revenge. He mentioned masks 'placed on living faces.' And he knew things about our family that few outsiders could."

Lorenzo's expression remained carefully neutral. "And what conclusions have you drawn from these cryptic statements?"

"That the official history of the Vinciguerra disappearance is a fabrication. That they didn't flee to Venice as exiles." Isabella turned to face her uncle directly. "That they died here in Florence, by Medici command, in some ritual involving those five masks we found designs for."

For a long moment, Lorenzo was silent, his gaze shifting to the serene effigy of his grandfather atop the tomb. When he finally spoke, his voice was low, almost reverent.

"History remembers Cosimo as the father of Florence's golden age—patron of arts, defender of republican values, humble merchant who never sought titles or crowns. What history forgets is what he sacrificed to secure that legacy."

"The Vinciguerra," Isabella whispered.

"Among others." Lorenzo gestured toward the chapel door. "Come. If you're to understand, you must see for yourself."

He led her not upward to his study, but down a narrow stone staircase behind the altar that Isabella had never noticed before. The steps descended far below the chapel, the air growing cooler and damper with each turn. Finally, they reached an iron-bound door that Lorenzo unlocked with a key kept on a chain around his neck.

"The true Medici archive," he explained, pushing the heavy door open. "Not the sanitized version upstairs that scholars and family members may access, but the actual record of our rise to power."

The chamber beyond was smaller than Isabella had expected, more a crypt than an archive. Stone walls glistened with moisture, and the only light came from a small oil lamp that Lorenzo ignited from the torch outside. Along the walls stood iron-bound chests and cabinets, each secured with multiple locks. In the center of the room, incongruously, sat a simple wooden table and two chairs.

"Few living souls have entered this room," Lorenzo said, placing the lamp on the table. "Myself, Giuliano, Michelozzi. Now you. Not even my wife knows of its existence."

Isabella felt the weight of this trust, even as part of her recoiled from what secrets might be contained in those locked chests.

Lorenzo approached one cabinet, unlocking it with another key from his collection. From within, he withdrew a leather-bound volume, its cover unmarked save for a small stamped symbol matching the five-petaled lily from Tornabuoni's desk.

"Cosimo's private journal," Lorenzo explained, placing it reverently on the table. "Not his public diaries that record political decisions and banking transactions, but his true thoughts—his fears, his doubts, and his most difficult choices."

As Lorenzo opened the journal to pages marked with silk ribbons, Isabella noticed something else: a small alcove in the far wall, partly concealed by shadow. Within it stood five small pedestals, each empty save for a thin layer of dust.

"What was displayed there?" she asked, pointing to the alcove.

Lorenzo glanced up, his expression darkening. "The masks. The originals. They were kept here as a reminder of the price paid for our ascendancy. They disappeared six months ago—the first sign that someone had breached our most secure sanctuary."

Isabella felt her blood chill. "Six months... just enough time for a skilled craftsman to create replicas."

"Precisely." Lorenzo beckoned her to the table. "Before I show you this record, I must know: are you prepared for the truth, Isabella? Some knowledge cannot be unlearned."

She met his gaze steadily. "I entered this path when I found the first feather, Uncle. I will see it through, whatever revelations await."

Lorenzo nodded solemnly and turned the journal so they both could read. The flowing script described events from October 1439 in Cosimo's own hand—a conspiracy uncovered, a threat to both family and republic that required decisive action. As Isabella read, horror grew within her like a poisonous vine.

"They were executed here? In our palazzo?" she whispered, unable to keep the shock from her voice.

"In the old stone chamber beneath the east wing—a room that predates even our ownership of this building." Lorenzo turned a page, revealing detailed diagrams of the five masks. "These were more than mere disguises. They were instruments."

Isabella read further, her hands beginning to tremble as she comprehended the full barbarity of what had occurred. The masks—crafted with hidden barbs and mechanisms designed to cause specific types of pain—had been placed on the five Vinciguerra men while they still lived. Each mask corresponded to a sin Cosimo believed they had committed against Florence and against divine order. Each was designed to extract a specific confession before death.

"This is monstrous," Isabella breathed, unable to continue reading.

"It was war," Lorenzo corrected quietly. "Not with armies, but with single families who controlled the destiny of thousands. The Vinciguerra would have destroyed everything—sold Florence to

Milan, executed every Medici down to the infants. Cosimo chose the lesser evil."

"And the girl?" Isabella asked, remembering the killer's words. "The one who witnessed it all?"

Lorenzo's face grew grave. "Lucia Vinciguerra. Eight years old. She was brought to identify her family members, to ensure we had captured all the conspirators. Cosimo never intended for her to witness the... procedure. But something went wrong. She saw everything."

Isabella closed her eyes, imagining the terror of a child forced to watch such brutality inflicted on her family. "What became of her?"

"Cosimo couldn't bring himself to harm her, despite the risk she posed. He placed her with a loyal family outside Florence, with a new name and identity. She grew up, married, even had children of her own—never knowing her true heritage." Lorenzo's voice had grown softer. "Or so we believed."

"And now one of her descendants hunts us," Isabella concluded. "With knowledge passed down in secret, or perhaps discovered only recently."

"Not a descendant," Lorenzo corrected grimly. "Lucia herself."

Isabella stared at her uncle in disbelief. "That's impossible. She would be an old woman now, over fifty years of age."

"Fifty-three," Lorenzo confirmed. "Still hale enough to orchestrate these murders, if not necessarily to commit them herself. The burned doll found with Bardi was identical to one Lucia carried the night she was taken from her family home. A doll my mother had commissioned specially for her—a peace offering between rival houses. Lucia would be the only one who could know of its significance."

The implications settled over Isabella like a shroud. "She wants us to experience the same terror her family felt. Five deaths for five masks."

"And the exposure of our family's darkest secret," Lorenzo added. "A secret that, if known, would destroy not just our power, but the very foundation of Florence's stability. The republic depends on Medici gold, Medici alliances, Medici legitimacy."

Lorenzo closed the journal with careful reverence. "Now you understand what we face. Not merely a killer, but the unraveling of everything our family has built over three generations."

Isabella's mind raced with connections, assembling the fragments into a coherent picture. "The pentagon—it's not just symbolic. It's a ritual recreation. The five points corresponding to the five deaths, arranged in the same pattern as the original executions."

Lorenzo nodded, a flicker of reluctant admiration crossing his features. "You see it clearly. Three points are established. Two remain to complete the pattern."

"And then what? What happens when the pentagon is complete?"

"According to old alchemical texts, a properly constructed pentagon becomes a doorway—a means of releasing energies normally contained." Lorenzo's voice took on an edge of concern. "Cosimo studied such matters extensively. He believed that the arrangement of the executions—the precise positioning of the victims and the masks they wore—created a kind of seal, binding the violence of that night within a mystical construct."

Isabella raised an eyebrow. "You cannot believe in such superstition, Uncle."

"I believe in patterns and their power," Lorenzo replied. "Whether mystical or merely psychological, the completion of this pentagon would represent the breaking of whatever containment Cosimo established. The final act in Lucia's vengeance."

A cold realization dawned on Isabella. "The last two victims... they must be Medici. The pattern demands it. That's why the killer hasn't struck directly at our family yet—he's saving us for the culmination."

"Yes." Lorenzo's face had become a mask of resolve. "Giuliano and myself, almost certainly. As the direct heirs of Cosimo's legacy, our deaths would complete the symmetry of her revenge."

Isabella felt fear tightening around her heart—not abstract dread, but immediate, personal terror for the two men who had been the constants of her life. "We must find her before the pattern can be completed."

"We will." Lorenzo stood, returning the journal to its cabinet. "Now that we know who we seek, della Torre can focus his search on a specific target—an aging woman of means, recently arrived in Florence or its environs."

As they prepared to leave the hidden chamber, Isabella paused at the alcove where the masks had once been displayed. "The man I spoke with last night... he was too young to be working alone. Lucia must have accomplices."

"Undoubtedly," Lorenzo agreed. "Perhaps her own children or grandchildren. The hatred of the Medici would have been her legacy to them, nurtured over decades."

Isabella thought of the stranger's intense dark eyes, the controlled precision of his movements. Not madness, but methodical purpose had driven him. "He knew the palazzo intimately. He moved through it like someone with memories of its corridors."

"A former servant, perhaps. Or someone who gained access through bribes and careful study." Lorenzo extinguished the lamp as they departed. "Regardless, he is a dead man walking. Della Torre's men will find him."

As they ascended the stairs back to the chapel, Isabella could not shake the image of the five empty pedestals, waiting like silent accusers for the masks to be returned. What would happen when the pentagon was complete? Would it merely signify the end of Lucia's vengeance, or was there something more—some final revelation or act yet concealed?

"Uncle," she said as they emerged into the chapel's tranquil light, "there's something I didn't tell you. About last night."

Lorenzo paused, regarding her with sudden wariness. "What is it?"

Isabella reached into her sleeve, withdrawing Tornabuoni's medallion. "He gave me this. Not as a threat, but as... a gift. He said it was being returned to its rightful circulation."

Lorenzo took the medallion, examining it with confused recognition. "This makes no sense. The medallion was indeed Tornabuoni's—I've seen him wear it countless times."

"He claimed it was originally Vinciguerra property. Stolen along with the five lives."

Lorenzo's brow furrowed as he turned the medallion over. "Impossible. This bears Tornabuoni's personal insignia, commissioned by his father decades ago." He pointed to markings on the reverse that Isabella hadn't noticed. "See these symbols? They represent the junction of the Arno and Mugnone rivers—the location of the first Tornabuoni banking venture."

"Then why would he claim it belonged to the Vinciguerra? Why take it specifically from Giovanni?" Isabella pressed.

"To confuse us. To make us doubt our own knowledge and history." Lorenzo pocketed the medallion with decision. "The killer plays mind games, Isabella. Remember that. Whatever he told you was calculated to sow uncertainty and division."

As they exited the chapel, the palazzo beyond hummed with activity. Guards patrolled in greater numbers than ever before, and messengers hurried to and from della Torre's makeshift command center in the eastern courtyard. The hunt for Lucia Vinciguerra had begun in earnest.

Yet Isabella could not dispel her unease. The stranger had seemed so certain, so persuasive in his conviction. What if there were truths even Lorenzo didn't know? What if Cosimo's journal contained only part of the story?

And most troubling of all—what if the danger lay not only in what was taken from the Medici, but in what had been hidden within their own walls for over forty years?

Chapter 8
The Artisan's Workshop

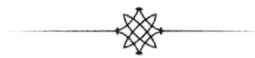

The search for Lucia Vinciguerra transformed Florence into an armed camp. Lorenzo's agents combed the city for any woman matching her description—now estimated to be in her early fifties, perhaps disguised or living under an assumed identity. Every inn, hostel, and rented apartment was investigated. Ships' manifests and city gate records from the past year were scrutinized for newcomers who might fit her profile.

Yet three days passed with no sign of the woman or her masked accomplice. The city held its breath, wondering where death would next appear.

Isabella had spent these days dividing her time between further research in the archives and accompanying Lorenzo to strategy meetings with della Torre and his lieutenants. The more she learned of the Vinciguerra affair, the more complex it appeared. The family had indeed been wealthy once, rivals to the early Medici banking ventures, but financial missteps had left them vulnerable by the time of Cosimo's rise to power. Their conspiracy with Milan seemed born more of desperation than ambition—a final, fatal attempt to reclaim lost prestige.

On the fourth morning, as Isabella reviewed property records from the 1430s, a detail caught her attention. The Vinciguerra had owned several properties in Florence, all confiscated after their "exile." Most had been sold or distributed to Medici allies, but one small workshop in the Oltrarno district appeared to have been overlooked in the redistribution—a leatherworker's studio once operated by a Vinciguerra retainer named Matteo Donati.

"Leatherworking," Isabella murmured to herself. "Like the masks..."

She summoned Michelozzi, who confirmed that the property had never been officially reassigned. "An oversight in the records, perhaps. The workshop was small, of little value compared to the Vinciguerra palazzo and lands."

"Or intentionally ignored," Isabella suggested. "Is there any record of this Donati after 1439?"

Michelozzi consulted another ledger. "None. He vanishes from the tax registries at the same time as his masters."

"Another victim of that night, unrecorded in even Cosimo's private journal?" Isabella wondered aloud. "Or perhaps an accomplice who escaped?"

"Speculation without evidence is dangerous, my lady," Michelozzi cautioned—his familiar refrain whenever Isabella's questions probed too deeply into uncomfortable history.

"Then let us gather evidence," she decided. "I want to see this workshop."

Michelozzi blanched. "Your uncle would never permit—"

"My uncle is occupied with the search for Lucia," Isabella countered. "This may be a meaningless detail, or it could be crucial. Either way, we lose nothing by investigating." Seeing his continued hesitation, she added, "I'll take guards, of course. And you, if you wish to accompany me."

The old secretary sighed, recognizing the stubborn determination he had witnessed in three generations of Medici. "I will arrange an escort. But we go only to observe from outside—no entering abandoned buildings without proper authority."

The Oltrarno district, south of the Arno River, had always been Florence's more bohemian quarter—home to artisans, craftsmen, and those whose fortunes had not yet risen enough to secure residences in the more prestigious northern precincts. Its narrow streets twisted between workshops and modest homes, the air filled with the sounds and smells of productive labor: the rhythmic hammering of metalworkers, the pungent odors of tanners and dyers, the sweet scents wafting from bakeries.

Isabella, Michelozzi, and four armed guards made their way through these streets, drawing curious glances from locals unaccustomed to Medici presence in their humble neighborhood. Following directions from ancient property records, they navigated to a small side street near Santo Spirito church.

"This should be it," Michelozzi indicated a narrow building wedged between a carpenter's shop and a spice merchant's store. Unlike its neighbors, which bustled with activity, this structure appeared abandoned—its windows shuttered, its door secured with rusted chains.

"It looks untouched since the Vinciguerra time," Isabella observed, studying the weathered facade. The stone lintel above the door bore a faded insignia—a craftsman's mark featuring intertwined tools that might once have identified Donati's workshop.

As they stood observing, an elderly woman emerged from the neighboring spice shop, eyeing them with the wary curiosity of someone who had witnessed enough Florentine politics to be suspicious of armed men in her street.

"Good day, grandmother," Isabella greeted her respectfully. "Might you know anything of this building? It appears long abandoned."

The woman squinted at Isabella, then at the workshop. "Abandoned, yes. But not unused." She lowered her voice conspiratorially. "Night visitors, these past months. Lights behind the shutters. Sounds of work."

Isabella felt a surge of excitement. "What kind of sounds?"

"Hammering. Scraping. Like someone working leather or parchment." The woman crossed herself. "Unnatural hours for honest labor. I told my son we should inform the night watch, but he said it wasn't our concern."

Isabella pressed a silver coin into the woman's gnarled hand. "You've been most helpful. One more question—have you seen who enters? A woman, perhaps? Or a man in fine clothes?"

The woman pocketed the coin with practiced swiftness. "A man, yes. Tall, lean as a winter wolf. Comes after midnight, leaves before dawn. Carries a satchel, always. Brown cloak, hood up even in warm weather." She hesitated. "And once, a woman. Older, but straight-backed. Arrived in a covered sedan chair, no markings. She wore widow's weeds, face veiled."

Isabella and Michelozzi exchanged glances. This matched what they sought—Lucia and her accomplice, using this forgotten family property as their workshop.

"When did you last see either of them?" Isabella asked.

"The man, three nights past. The woman, not since last week." The old shopkeeper leaned closer. "Are they criminals? Counterfeiters, perhaps?"

"Something of that nature," Isabella replied diplomatically. "You've done Florence a service, grandmother. Should you see either again, send word to the palazzo. There would be further reward."

As the woman retreated to her shop, Michelozzi tugged at Isabella's sleeve. "We should return immediately. Inform the captain, let his men handle this."

Isabella studied the chained door, noticing subtle details—the chains, though rusted on the surface, showed signs of regular movement where they passed through the door handles. The shutters, seemingly firmly closed, had minute gaps where the wood had been carefully shaved to allow them to open without appearing disturbed from the street.

"Someone has gone to great lengths to make this place appear abandoned while maintaining access," she observed. "I doubt della Torre's men would notice such subtleties in a neighborhood raid."

"Nevertheless, this is a task for armed men, not—"

"We have armed men," Isabella interrupted, nodding to their escort. "Four of Lorenzo's finest. Surely that suffices to explore an artisan's workshop?"

Before Michelozzi could object further, Isabella approached the guards. "We need to examine this building's interior. Can the chains be removed without damaging the door?"

The captain of her escort, a veteran named Orsini, assessed the lock. "Easily, my lady. But the secretary is right—protocol demands we report this to Captain della Torre before proceeding."

"Time is against us," Isabella argued. "Every day, more lives hang in the balance. If this is indeed where the killer crafts his instruments, we might find evidence of his next targets."

The guards exchanged uncomfortable glances, torn between proper procedure and the authority of a Medici command.

Finally, Orsini nodded. "We'll enter, but with caution. You and the secretary remain outside until we've secured the space."

This compromise satisfied Isabella, who watched impatiently as the guards made short work of the chains. The door opened with surprising silence, its hinges recently oiled—further evidence of ongoing use. The guards disappeared inside, weapons drawn.

Minutes later, Orsini emerged. "All clear, my lady. The space appears abandoned, but as you suspected, shows signs of recent activity."

Isabella entered with Michelozzi reluctantly trailing behind. The workshop's front room was sparse—empty tables, shelves stripped of tools, a layer of undisturbed dust covering most surfaces. But toward the back, a different scene emerged. A large workbench had been cleared and cleaned, illuminated by a skylight partially obscured with cloth to prevent light from being visible from the street at night.

Upon this bench lay evidence of the killer's preparations: sketches of masks in various stages of design, leather scraps in different states of treatment, and most disturbingly, anatomical drawings showing precise points on the human head where the masks' hidden mechanisms would cause maximum pain with minimal visible damage.

"These are the work of a trained mind," Isabella murmured, examining the anatomical sketches. "Someone with medical knowledge."

"Or a torturer's expertise," Michelozzi added grimly.

The guards had spread through the space, examining its contents with professional thoroughness. "My lady," one called from a small back room. "You should see this."

Isabella entered what appeared to have been a storage area, now transformed into a different kind of workshop. The walls were covered with maps of Florence—detailed street plans marked with routes, guard positions, and schedules for patrol rotations. Five locations had been circled in red ink, connected by lines to form a perfect pentagon across the city map.

"The murder sites," Isabella realized. "Three completed, two planned."

The first three circles corresponded exactly to where the victims had been found. The fourth marked a location near the Ponte Vecchio—the old bridge lined with shops and residences. The fifth and final point fell directly on the Medici palazzo itself.

"The pattern concludes where it began," Michelozzi whispered. "The final killing is planned for your home."

But something else on the wall had captured Isabella's attention—a portrait, rendered in exquisite detail despite its small size. It showed a young girl with solemn eyes and a serious expression beyond her years. She held a small doll crafted in the image of a courtly lady, identical to the burned doll found with Bardi's body.

"Lucia," Isabella breathed. "Painted before the night of masks."

Beside this portrait hung another, clearly made by the same hand but decades later—showing the same subject as a mature woman, her childhood solemnity hardened into something colder and more resolute. The resemblance was unmistakable despite the passage of years.

"These were painted recently," Isabella noted, touching the edge of the newer portrait. "The oils are still not fully cured."

"A shrine to revenge," Michelozzi murmured. "Forty years in the making."

As they continued examining the room, a guard called from another corner. "Documents, my lady. Many of them."

On a small writing desk lay stacks of parchment—letters, diagrams, and what appeared to be personal journals dating back decades. Isabella approached, recognizing their value immediately. "These could contain everything—Lucia's whereabouts, her accomplices, her next moves."

Before she could examine them further, a muffled sound from outside caught their attention—the rapid approach of hoofbeats, then men's voices raised in command. Orsini moved quickly to the window, peering through a crack in the shutters.

"City guards," he reported. "At least a dozen, led by Captain della Torre himself."

Michelozzi looked pointedly at Isabella. "It seems someone informed them of our unauthorized expedition."

"Gather the documents," Isabella instructed the guards. "Quickly. And that portrait of the older woman—we need della Torre to distribute her likeness to his men."

As the guards hurried to comply, the front door burst open. Della Torre entered, his expression thunderous when he caught sight of Isabella.

"Lady Isabella," he acknowledged stiffly. "Your uncle was... concerned when he learned of your departure from the palazzo without his knowledge."

"Fortune favors the bold, Captain," she replied smoothly. "We've discovered the killer's workshop and planning room. See for yourself." She gestured to the wall of maps and the workbench with its disturbing designs.

Della Torre surveyed the space with a professional eye, his anger giving way to grudging approval. "Indeed, an important discovery. Though protocol exists for good reason, my lady."

"Protocol would have given them time to clear this space," Isabella countered. "Already we arrived barely in time—it appears they've begun removing evidence." She indicated empty spaces on the workbench where dust patterns suggested recently removed objects.

The captain nodded to his men, who began a more thorough search of the premises. "The Magnificent One requests your immediate return to the palazzo," he told Isabella. "I'm to escort you personally."

"Of course. But first, show him what we've found." She handed della Torre the portrait of the older Lucia. "This is our quarry—Lucia Vinciguerra as she appears now. Distribute copies to every guard and informant in the city."

As della Torre examined the portrait, one of his men emerged from the back room holding something wrapped in cloth. "Captain, we found this concealed beneath the floorboards."

He unwrapped the object carefully, revealing a mask—not one of the theatrical faces used in the murders, but something far more disturbing. This mask was crafted of human skin, yellowed and preserved through some arcane process, stretched over a frame of wire and wood. It bore no adornment, no artistic flourishes—just the preserved features of a man, frozen in an expression of agony.

"God in heaven," Michelozzi whispered, crossing himself.

Della Torre's face hardened as he studied the grotesque object. "Do we know whose face this was?"

"The craftsmanship suggests Donati's work," Isabella said, fighting to keep her voice steady. "And if the pattern holds, this would be one of the original masks—made from one of the Vinciguerra five."

"A family heirloom of the most macabre kind," della Torre observed grimly. "Preserved as a reminder and template for the current killings."

As the guards continued their search, uncovering more disturbing evidence of the plot's elaborate preparation, Isabella felt a chill of certainty. Whatever had begun on that October night in 1439 had never truly ended—not for Lucia, who had built her entire life around this moment of vengeance. The masks, the pentagon, the careful selection of victims—all led inexorably toward a final confrontation that would either break the Medici or cement their power for another generation.

And at the center of it all stood the question no one had yet answered: what had really happened to Lucia after she witnessed her family's destruction? What experiences had transformed a traumatized child into the architect of such methodical revenge?

The answers, Isabella suspected, lay not in this workshop of horrors, but in the hidden places of her own family's legacy—truths buried deeper than even Lorenzo might know.

Chapter 9
The Conspiracy Unravels

The Medici palazzo had transformed into a fortress. Guards stood three deep at every entrance, while archers patrolled the rooftops with vigilant eyes scanning the surrounding streets. Inside, the usual bustle of courtiers and petitioners had been replaced by an atmosphere of tense anticipation. Lorenzo had dismissed all non-essential staff and restricted access to the family wing to a handful of trusted servants.

In Lorenzo's private study, the evidence gathered from the workshop lay spread across tables—maps, sketches, anatomical drawings, and most valuable of all, Lucia's journals. Isabella had spent hours poring over these personal records, piecing together the shattered fragments of a life consumed by vengeance.

"She was adopted by the Donati family," Isabella explained to Lorenzo and Giuliano, who stood examining the map with its ominous pentagon. "Matteo Donati—the leatherworker who crafted the original masks—escaped the purge with Lucia. They fled to Padua, not Venice as our records claimed, where he raised her as his daughter while teaching her his craft."

"A traumatized child raised by the man who helped torture her family," Giuliano observed grimly. "One can hardly imagine a more perfect crucible for hatred."

"There's more," Isabella continued, turning pages in the journal. "Lucia married at seventeen—a physician named Paolo Conti. He taught her anatomy and the medicinal properties of various compounds. Their son, Marco, was born in 1447."

Lorenzo's expression darkened. "The masked man you encountered at the ball."

"Almost certainly," Isabella agreed. "The timing fits—he appeared to be in his early thirties. According to these entries, Lucia trained him from childhood in the 'family purpose,' as she calls it. Every aspect of his education was designed toward a single goal: the execution of this revenge."

"An entire life dedicated to our destruction," Giuliano murmured, almost admiringly. "Such devotion, however twisted, commands a certain respect."

Lorenzo shot his brother a sharp glance. "Save your admiration for those who build rather than destroy, brother." He turned back to Isabella. "What else have you learned from these writings?"

"They returned to Florence only six months ago, after decades of preparation. Lucia had amassed considerable wealth through her husband's practice and careful investments—all to fund this final act of retribution." Isabella hesitated before adding, "She appears to have infiltrated our household. There are detailed observations of palazzo routines that could only come from someone with regular access."

"A servant," Lorenzo concluded. "Or someone posing as one."

"I've already begun reviewing all staff hired within the past year," Michelozzi interjected from his position by the door. "Particularly those with access to the family quarters."

Isabella closed the journal, her expression troubled. "There's something else, something that doesn't align with what we know. Throughout these writings, Lucia repeatedly refers to something called 'the sixth mask'—a final instrument of justice that would reveal, in her words, 'the truth that would destroy the Medici more thoroughly than any blade.'"

"Six masks?" Giuliano frowned. "All our records speak of five—one for each Vinciguerra heir."

"Exactly." Isabella turned to Lorenzo. "What was the sixth mask, Uncle? What secret remains hidden even from your knowledge?"

Lorenzo's face betrayed nothing, but Isabella noticed his knuckles whitening where he gripped the edge of the table. "A phantom. A fiction created by a disturbed mind to justify her crusade."

Before Isabella could press further, Captain della Torre entered, his expression grave. "My lord, a messenger arrived from the Ponte Vecchio. Piero Guicciardini was found dead in his jeweler's shop not thirty minutes ago."

The room fell silent. Guicciardini—one of Florence's wealthiest gold merchants and a longtime Medici ally—represented the fourth point in the killer's pentagon.

"How?" Lorenzo demanded.

"Strangled with a gold chain of his own making," della Torre reported. "The crimson feather was left pinned to his tongue. And there was a mask—"

"Hanging above him," Isabella finished. "With distinctive features representing greed or avarice."

Della Torre nodded, unsurprised by her insight. "The shop was locked from within. No witnesses saw anyone enter or leave."

"And the message?" Lorenzo asked.

"Written on parchment in red ink: 'Four debts paid. One remains. The circle closes where blood first spilled. Tonight, the Magnificent One will face the sixth face of truth.'" Della Torre paused before adding, "It was signed with a name: Lucia Vinciguerra."

Giuliano paced the room, tension radiating from his athletic frame. "She abandons subterfuge. This is her declaration of final intent."

"She believes victory is within her grasp," Lorenzo observed coldly. "A confidence we must shatter." He turned to della Torre. "The palazzo must be sealed completely. No one enters or leaves until morning—not servants, not messengers, not even members of the Signoria. Post triple guards at every known entrance, and search for unknown ones."

"What of the Ponte Vecchio site?" the captain asked.

"Leave men to secure it, but focus your forces here. The palazzo is her final target—this room, specifically." Lorenzo pointed to the map where the fifth point of the pentagon centered precisely on his private study.

As della Torre departed to implement these orders, Lorenzo turned to his brother and niece. "We have perhaps twelve hours before she makes her attempt. Giuliano, arm yourself and stay with me. Isabella, you will retreat to the secure chamber beneath the chapel with Michelozzi. Take these documents—continue searching for any detail that might reveal her method of attack."

Isabella stood her ground. "I would be more useful here, Uncle. I've studied her writings more thoroughly than anyone—I might recognize her patterns or intentions."

"This is not a scholarly exercise, child," Lorenzo replied sharply. "When Marco Conti enters this palazzo—and he will find a way—he comes to kill, not debate."

"All the more reason to have every advantage at hand," Isabella countered. "Including my insights."

Brother and niece locked eyes in a contest of wills that Giuliano observed with barely concealed amusement. Finally, Lorenzo relented slightly.

"You may remain until dusk. Then you go below with Michelozzi—no arguments. I'll not have three generations of Medici at risk in the same chamber."

As the day progressed, tension mounted within the palazzo. Servants moved through the corridors only in pairs, accompanied by guards. Every window was secured, every chimney and drain examined for possible entry points. Lorenzo conducted the defense like a military campaign, deploying men with strategic precision while continuing to review the evidence from Lucia's workshop.

By late afternoon, Isabella had completed her examination of the journals, yet crucial questions remained unanswered. The "sixth mask" was mentioned repeatedly without explanation, and there were oblique references to "the truth in the blood" that defied clear interpretation.

As shadows lengthened across Florence, Lorenzo summoned his closest advisors for final preparations. Isabella, despite the approaching deadline for her removal to safety, had persuaded her uncle to allow her presence. They gathered in Lorenzo's study—the likely target of the coming attack—to review what was known and unknown.

"The pattern is clear," Poliziano observed, studying the map. "Four deaths forming precise points of a pentagon, with this room as the fifth point. Each victim connected to your family, each killed in a manner reflecting their supposed sins."

"But what happens when the pattern is complete?" Giuliano wondered. "Beyond the obvious threat to Lorenzo's life, what does Lucia hope to achieve?"

Isabella, who had been unusually quiet, finally spoke. "Revelation. The pentagon is not merely a pattern of deaths—it's a ritual of disclosure." She looked up from Lucia's journal. "She believes that when the fifth death occurs at the final point, something will be revealed that destroys the Medici more thoroughly than any physical attack could."

"What could possibly hold such power?" Giuliano scoffed. "Florence has weathered Medici scandals before. The Pazzi conspiracy failed despite assassinating your brother in the cathedral itself. What secret could be worse than open murder in a house of God?"

A somber silence fell over the room. Giuliano had rarely spoken so directly of his twin brother's death five years earlier—a wound in the family that had never fully healed.

"Perhaps the question is not what secret," Isabella said carefully, "but whose." She turned to Lorenzo. "Uncle, these journals contain repeated references to something Lucia calls 'the girl's truth.' Not her truth—the girl's truth. As though it concerns someone else."

Lorenzo's expression remained impassive, but Isabella caught a flicker of something in his eyes—not fear, exactly, but a wary recognition.

"Speculations without evidence are dangerous," he replied, echoing Michelozzi's frequent caution. "Focus on what we know, not what we conjecture."

Before Isabella could press further, a guard burst into the room. "My lords, Lady Clarice requests immediate audience. She says it concerns the family's safety."

Lorenzo nodded, and moments later his wife entered, her normally composed features taut with concern. In her hand she clutched a small package wrapped in silk.

"This was delivered to my chamber by one of the kitchen boys," she announced without preamble. "He claimed a hooded pilgrim at the service entrance paid him to bring it directly to me, bypassing all other hands."

"The boy is being questioned?" Lorenzo asked sharply.

"By della Torre himself," Clarice confirmed. "But the package... I believe you should see its contents immediately."

She unwrapped the silk to reveal a small wooden box carved with the now-familiar five-petaled lily. Inside lay a folded parchment and a single object: a silver thimble, identical to the one sent earlier but for one detail—this one was stained with what appeared to be dried blood.

"A second thimble," Isabella murmured. "I thought the first was unique."

"It was," Lorenzo said quietly. "This is the same thimble, returned with new significance." He unfolded the parchment and read aloud:

"'The blood of innocents stains all Medici hands. Tonight, the circle closes. Tonight, the sixth face speaks. Ask your wife about the girl child born in shadow. Ask about the daughter whose blood was mixed with yours by your own father's command.'"

All eyes turned to Clarice, whose face had drained of color. "Lies," she whispered. "Vicious, twisted lies meant to divide us when unity is most needed."

"Of course," Lorenzo agreed, too quickly. He refolded the parchment with careful precision. "A transparent attempt to create discord on the eve of her attack."

But Isabella had caught something in the exchange between husband and wife—a current of unspoken communication, a shared knowledge that excluded others in the room.

"The girl child born in shadow," she repeated slowly. "Could this refer to Lucia herself? Perhaps some connection to our family that would explain the intensity of this vendetta?"

"Enough speculation," Lorenzo declared with finality. "Night approaches, and with it, danger. Clarice, return to your chambers and remain there under guard. Giuliano, assemble our most trusted men in the antechamber. Isabella, the time has come for you to retreat to safety with Michelozzi."

His tone brooked no further argument. Isabella reluctantly gathered Lucia's journals, preparing to depart for the secure chamber beneath the chapel. As she reached the door, she turned back.

"Uncle, whatever secret Lucia Vinciguerra believes will destroy our family—truth or falsehood—you need not face it alone. The strength of the Medici has always been our unity, not our secrets."

Lorenzo's expression softened momentarily. "Your father would be proud of the woman you've become, Isabella. Now go—keep safe the knowledge you've gathered. If this night goes poorly, you may be the only one left to ensure the family's survival."

With these ominous words echoing in her mind, Isabella descended with Michelozzi to the hidden chamber beneath the chapel. Two guards were posted outside the iron-bound door, with orders to admit no one without Lorenzo's personal command.

Inside, oil lamps cast flickering shadows across the stone walls. Michelozzi arranged the documents on the central table, his gnarled hands moving with practiced efficiency despite his obvious anxiety.

"We should continue searching for insights that might help your uncle," he suggested, selecting one of Lucia's journals. "Though I fear the crucial moment approaches too quickly for our discoveries to matter."

Isabella nodded absently, her mind still churning with the implications of the message delivered to Clarice. The reference to a girl child born in shadow had struck a chord deep within her—a half-remembered conversation overheard years ago, something concerning her own father's early life.

"Michelozzi," she said suddenly, "what do you know of my father's birth? Were there any unusual circumstances?"

The old secretary froze momentarily, then resumed his organization of documents with too-careful precision. "Lord Giovanni was born in 1421, the second son of Cosimo and Contessina. A normal birth by all accounts."

"By all accounts," Isabella repeated. "But were there other accounts? Unofficial ones?"

Michelozzi's expression closed like a shutter against rain. "Lady Isabella, these are matters long settled into history. Your focus should remain on the present threat."

"The present threat centers on a secret from that exact period," Isabella countered. "The early 1420s—when my father was born, when the Vinciguerra were still powerful in Florence. What connects these families beyond political rivalry? What blood was 'mixed' as the message claimed?"

Michelozzi remained silent, but his discomfort was palpable. Isabella changed tactics.

"You've served my family for over fifty years, longer than I've been alive. Your loyalty has never wavered." She leaned forward, her voice softening. "That loyalty now demands truth, not protection. Whatever Lucia knows or believes, it will be revealed tonight one way or another. Better we understand it first, to defend against its power."

The secretary's ancient eyes studied her face, weighing decades of oaths against present necessity. Finally, he sighed—a sound of capitulation.

"There were... rumors," he began reluctantly. "Never recorded, barely whispered even among the most trusted circle. In 1420, when Contessina was struggling to provide Cosimo a second son, a solution was arranged."

"What solution?" Isabella pressed, her heart quickening.

"A young woman of suitable background but diminished circumstances was brought to a Medici country villa. She remained there, in seclusion, until she delivered a male child in the summer of 1421. That child was presented to Florence as Contessina's son—your father, Giovanni."

Isabella stared at the old man, struggling to absorb this revelation. "My grandmother was not Contessina de' Bardi? My father was... illegitimate?"

"Not illegitimate," Michelozzi corrected quickly. "Cosimo was indeed his father. But his mother was not the woman history records. Such arrangements were not uncommon among great families facing succession challenges."

"Who was she?" Isabella asked. "This unknown grandmother of mine?"

Michelozzi looked away, unable to meet her gaze. "That was the most closely guarded secret of all. For she was not entirely 'suitable background' as the story claimed. She was..." He faltered.

"Lucia Vinciguerra's mother," Isabella whispered, the pieces suddenly aligning with terrible clarity. "My father and Lucia shared a mother. They were half-siblings."

Michelozzi nodded slowly. "Maria Vinciguerra—youngest daughter of the family patriarch. Beautiful, intelligent, and deemed expendable when her family's fortunes began to falter. She was given to Cosimo as part of a complex financial arrangement—a human token in exchange for extended credit."

Isabella felt her world shifting beneath her feet. "So when Cosimo ordered the execution of the Vinciguerra heirs, he was ordering the death of his son's uncles. And Lucia..."

"Was your father's niece," Michelozzi finished. "Cosimo never knew of her existence. Maria died in childbirth with Lucia, who was raised secretly among her mother's family. By the time Cosimo discovered this branch of the Vinciguerra line, the child had vanished into obscurity."

"Until now," Isabella breathed. "She returns not just for vengeance, but to claim her birthright. 'The truth in the blood'—she means our shared bloodline. The Vinciguerra blood that flows in Medici veins."

"In your veins," Michelozzi corrected gently. "You alone, of the current generation, carry this mixed heritage. Your father was half Vinciguerra, making you one-quarter their blood."

Isabella sat heavily in her chair, the weight of this revelation pressing upon her like a physical force. "That's why the masked man—Marco—singled me out at the ball. Not to threaten, but to recognize. He called me cousin."

"A relationship he would value far differently than you," Michelozzi warned. "To him, it represents legitimacy for his mother's claim. To Florence, should it become known..."

He didn't need to finish. Isabella understood the implications all too well. Florence prided itself on the purity of its leading families. The revelation that Medici power was built upon Vinciguerra blood—that the supposedly distinct bloodlines were in fact intertwined—would undermine the very foundation of Lorenzo's authority.

"The sixth mask," Isabella said suddenly. "It's not a physical object—it's a metaphor. The final unmasking is the revelation of this truth."

A distant commotion filtered down from above—shouts, running footsteps. The attack on the palazzo had begun.

"We must warn Lorenzo," Isabella declared, rising. "Whatever Lucia plans, this knowledge might help him counter it."

Michelozzi moved to block the door. "Your uncle ordered us to remain here until morning, regardless of what we might hear."

"That was before we understood the true nature of the threat," Isabella argued. "Lucia doesn't just want Lorenzo's death—she wants his legacy destroyed, his family line revealed as partially her own. She wants Florence to know that Medici rule has always been built on Vinciguerra foundations."

The old secretary wavered, torn between contradictory loyalties. Above them, the sounds of conflict intensified.

"If Lorenzo falls without this knowledge, all is lost," Isabella pressed. "If he survives but the truth emerges without preparation, the damage to our family could be irreparable. I must reach him, Michelozzi. Now."

Finally, the secretary nodded. "There is another way out—a passage known only to the family archivists." He moved to a seemingly solid wall and pressed a specific stone. A section of the wall swung inward, revealing a narrow corridor. "It leads to your uncle's private oratory. From there, you can reach his study unseen."

Isabella gathered the most relevant journals and documents. "You remain here. If I fail to return by dawn, take these evidence to the Signoria. Ensure that whatever happens tonight, some version of the truth survives—preferably one that preserves what can be saved of our family's honor."

"God go with you, Lady Isabella," Michelozzi said gravely. "The fate of Florence may rest on your success."

With these sobering words echoing in her mind, Isabella entered the secret passage, ascending toward whatever deadly confrontation awaited above.

Chapter 10
Trap at the Cathedral

The narrow passage wound upward through the palazzo's stone foundations, a claustrophobic ascent illuminated only by the small oil lamp Michelozzi had pressed into Isabella's hand. Cobwebs brushed her face, and the air hung thick with dust. Clearly, this route had not been traveled in years.

As she climbed, the sounds of conflict above grew more distinct—shouts, the clash of weapons, running footsteps. After what seemed an eternity, the passage ended at a small wooden door leading into Lorenzo's private oratory. Isabella extinguished her lamp and moved to the connecting door, easing it open to peer into the study.

The scene that greeted her froze her blood.

Lorenzo sat at his desk, unharmed but unnaturally still. Across from him stood Lucia Vinciguerra in a gown of deep crimson, her silver-streaked black hair falling loose down her back. Despite her fifty-three years, she stood commanding, one hand resting on Marco's shoulder. Giuliano knelt on the floor with a thin blade pressed against his throat by a guard wearing Medici colors—a traitor within their ranks.

"The hour grows late, Magnifico," Lucia was saying. "Your men fight the wrong battle. The true contest is here, between us, as it has always been between our families."

"What do you want, Lucia?" Lorenzo asked, his voice steady despite the danger.

"Want?" She laughed—a sound like glass breaking. "What I wanted died forty years ago in your grandfather's torture chamber. What I want now is completion. Justice, served cold after decades of waiting."

"Justice for your family's conspiracy against Florence?" Lorenzo challenged. "They plotted treason. Their fate, while harsh, was the consequence of their actions."

"Their actions?" Lucia stepped closer, her face terrible in its controlled rage. "What action justified flaying the skin from my brothers' faces while they still lived? What treason deserved having their screams preserved in masks of their own flesh? I was eight years old when your grandfather forced me to watch what a banking dynasty does to its rivals."

Isabella winced at the horror in Lucia's words. The journals had described the torture, but hearing it spoken by the child witness herself made the barbarity freshly immediate.

"Not vengeance. Revelation," Lucia continued, gesturing to Marco, who produced a document. "This is why you will die tonight. Not for what your grandfather did to my family, but for what your family has hidden from Florence for three generations."

Marco began to read: "I, Cosimo de' Medici, acknowledge that on this day, the feast of Saint John the Baptist in the year of our Lord 1421, a male child born of my union with Maria Vinciguerra shall henceforth be recognized as my legitimate son and heir, Giovanni de' Medici..."

Isabella stifled a gasp. The document confirmed exactly what Michelozzi had revealed—with a crucial difference. This was no secret arrangement, but a formal acknowledgment of legitimacy.

"And what do you intend to do with this supposed proof?" Lorenzo asked.

"Distribute copies throughout Florence by dawn," Marco answered. "By midday, all will know that Medici power is built on Vinciguerra blood—that the family your grandfather tortured were your own father's uncles. That the Medici line is tainted with the same blood you deemed unworthy to live."

"Florence has weathered greater scandals," Lorenzo scoffed, though Isabella saw tension in his shoulders.

"But will it weather this as well?" Lucia produced a second document. "The full account of that October night—the methods employed, the children made to watch, the unholy ritual aspects that transformed murder into something far darker. Cosimo did not merely kill my family. He enacted a pagan rite designed to transfer their power to Medici hands."

At this, even Lorenzo's composure wavered.

"I merely need to suggest such things," Lucia said with cold satisfaction. "In a city already suspicious of your family's rise to power, these seeds will find fertile ground."

She turned back to Lorenzo. "However, I am not without mercy. There is an alternative."

"Name it," Lorenzo said flatly.

"Abdicate your position. Withdraw from Florence with your immediate family. Leave the republic to govern itself truly. In exchange, these documents remain sealed."

Isabella could see her uncle calculating possibilities with the same precision he applied to banking ledgers. The offer was not without logic—Medici power preserved, if diminished and removed from Florence.

"And what guarantee would I have?" Lorenzo asked.

"My word," Lucia replied simply. "Which, unlike Medici promises, has never been broken."

A tense silence filled the chamber. Isabella knew she should reveal herself, but something held her back—an instinct that the scene before her was not all it appeared.

Her instinct proved correct when Lorenzo's expression suddenly shifted from contemplation to triumph. "I admire your planning, Lucia. But like your family before you, you've overlooked a critical detail."

He made a small gesture with his right hand. Instantly, the supposedly traitorous guard shifted his blade toward Marco, who barely dodged the attack. Simultaneously, the study's side doors burst open, revealing Captain della Torre and six armed men who had been waiting in concealment.

"You've been expected, Lucia Vinciguerra," Lorenzo announced, rising from his desk. "Did you truly believe you could enter the heart of Medici power without my knowledge? That a single turned guard represents the extent of my household loyalty?"

Marco had drawn his own blade, backing toward his mother. "We are not defeated yet."

"You were defeated before you began," Lorenzo countered. "The difference is that I offer what Cosimo did not—the chance to live out your lives in exile rather than ending them here."

"Seize them," Lorenzo ordered his men. "The documents as well."

As della Torre's guards moved forward, Lucia began to laugh—not the bitter sound from before, but genuine amusement that stopped the advancing men.

"Oh, Lorenzo," she said, wiping tears of mirth from her eyes. "You always were the cleverest of your family. But cleverness is not wisdom."

With a sudden movement, she smashed a small glass vial against the floor. Thick white smoke billowed upward with unnatural speed, filling the chamber and sending the guards into a coughing frenzy.

Isabella covered her mouth with her sleeve, squinting through the rapidly spreading fog. Then, directly before her hiding place, the connecting door was flung fully open. Marco stood there, his eyes meeting hers with recognition.

"Come, cousin," he said, extending his hand. "This is no place for you."

Before Isabella could respond, Lucia appeared beside her son. "Isabella de' Medici," she acknowledged. "The one untainted branch of a poisoned tree. Come with us. Learn the full truth of your heritage—not the sanitized version your uncle permits you to discover."

"To what end?" Isabella demanded. "More death? More revenge?"

"Justice," Marco corrected. "And perhaps, renewal. Florence deserves better than endless Medici dominion."

"Choose now," Lucia urged. "Remain in gilded ignorance or embrace the fullness of your blood—both Medici and Vinciguerra."

Isabella hesitated, torn between family loyalty and the pull of concealed truths. But before she could decide, the smoke began to clear, revealing della Torre advancing with drawn sword.

"Flee or stay, the choice is yours," Marco said urgently. "But know this—tonight was merely a declaration, not our final move."

With that, he and Lucia slipped away through another hidden passage that Isabella hadn't known existed. Della Torre reached her a moment later, surprised to find her there.

"Lady Isabella! Are you harmed?"

"No," she managed, her mind still reeling. "Where is my uncle?"

The smoke had dissipated enough to reveal Lorenzo being attended to by Giuliano, both disoriented but unharmed.

"They've escaped," Lorenzo rasped. "And the documents?"

"Gone with them," Giuliano confirmed grimly.

Isabella stepped fully into the study. "Uncle, I must speak with you. There are truths about our family that cannot remain hidden if we are to counter this threat effectively."

Lorenzo studied his niece, noting the documents clutched in her hands—Lucia's journals from the hidden chamber.

"Clear the room," he ordered. "Giuliano, remain. Captain, secure the palazzo."

As the guards withdrew, Lorenzo turned back to Isabella. "So, niece. How much have you discovered on your own?"

"Enough," she replied steadily. "I know of my grandmother Maria Vinciguerra. I know my father was half their blood, making me part Vinciguerra as well."

Lorenzo exchanged a look with Giuliano before sighing—a rare display of fatigue.

"I had hoped to spare you this knowledge," he said quietly. "Not out of deception, but protection."

"I'm stronger than you think," Isabella countered. "And knowledge, however painful, is preferable to ignorance."

Lorenzo indicated a chair, which Isabella took, placing Lucia's journals on the desk between them.

"The truth, then," Lorenzo began. "Maria Vinciguerra was indeed your grandmother—a beautiful, intelligent woman from a family in financial decline. The union with Cosimo was arranged to satisfy mutual needs: the Medici required a second son, the Vinciguerra needed financial support."

"What became of her?" Isabella asked.

"She died giving birth to Lucia in 1431," Lorenzo continued. "By then, relations between the families had soured. The Vinciguerra blamed Cosimo for Maria's death. They began their conspiracy with Milan shortly thereafter."

"And when Cosimo discovered this plot?"

Lorenzo's expression hardened. "He acted to preserve Florence from foreign domination and the Medici from destruction. The methods employed were... extreme by today's standards."

"The ritual aspects Lucia mentioned," Isabella pressed. "Were those real?"

"Cosimo was fascinated by ancient wisdom," Lorenzo admitted. "The execution incorporated elements of hermetic ritual—creating a psychological seal upon the act."

"The masks," Isabella said, trying to comprehend the horror. "They were made from..."

"Yes," Lorenzo confirmed grimly. "The masks were both execution and memorial, ensuring the Vinciguerra threat was literally contained."

"And the child Lucia was forced to witness this?"

"An error in execution," Lorenzo said, his voice tightening. "The girl was meant only to identify her kinsmen, then be removed. By the time Cosimo realized she had seen everything, the damage was done."

Isabella processed this information. "And now she returns, with proof of our shared bloodline and evidence of Cosimo's ritual executions."

"It would devastate Medici authority," Lorenzo finished. "Not just in Florence, but throughout Italy."

"What will you do?" Isabella asked.

"What I must. Defend our family and, by extension, Florence itself."

"From justice?" Isabella challenged softly.

"From chaos," Lorenzo corrected. "The Medici represent stability. If we fall, Florence falls with us."

"They will strike again," Giuliano observed. "Lucia has waited forty years—she will not abandon her purpose now."

Lorenzo nodded. "Her approach must change. Having failed at direct assault, she will seek a more public venue for her revelation."

"The Duomo," Isabella said, remembering the map from the workshop. "The cathedral was marked on her plans. Tomorrow is Easter Sunday."

"The perfect audience for Lucia's revelation," Lorenzo concluded grimly. "She means to expose our family before God and Florence together."

Isabella leaned forward. "Then we must intercept her, not with guards and swords, but with a counter-truth that defuses her revelation."

"A trap," Giuliano suggested, his tactical mind engaging. "We know where she plans to appear."

Lorenzo rose, decision made. "Captain della Torre will coordinate with the cathedral guards. We'll establish a perimeter subtle enough not to disrupt the Easter service but tight enough to ensure no unauthorized persons approach the pulpit."

"She'll anticipate such measures," Isabella cautioned.

"Which is why you will be our key piece," Lorenzo said. "Lucia and her son have a particular interest in you, Isabella. They see you as potentially sympathetic due to your shared bloodline."

Isabella stiffened. "You would use me as bait?"

"You alone might draw them into conversation rather than immediate action."

The strategy was logical, Isabella had to admit, though it placed her in considerable danger.

"I'll do it," she declared. "But on one condition."

Lorenzo's expression became guarded. "Name it."

"When this is resolved, no more secrets within our family. The selective truths, the hidden histories—they've created the very vulnerability Lucia exploits."

Lorenzo and Giuliano exchanged glances laden with unspoken communication before Lorenzo finally agreed, with one caveat: "Though such openness must remain within family boundaries. The world receives only what truths serve Florence's interests."

It was a compromise, but Isabella recognized it as the most her pragmatic uncle would concede. She nodded her acceptance.

"Then let us prepare for Easter morning," she said. "And pray that Florence's cathedral sees revelation rather than bloodshed."

Chapter 11
Isabella's Discovery

The private chamber adjacent to Lorenzo's study had been cleared of all but the essential participants in this unexpected negotiation. Isabella sat beside her uncle, facing Lucia and Marco across a table of polished oak that gleamed in the afternoon light. Captain della Torre stood guard at the door, the only other person permitted to witness this extraordinary meeting.

The journey from cathedral to palazzo had been tense but uneventful, conducted with such discretion that few in Florence realized the architect of recent murders now sat in the heart of Medici power. Lorenzo had received news of Isabella's intervention with characteristic adaptability—his initial anger at her unauthorized action quickly giving way to calculated assessment of the opportunity it presented.

"The documents," Lorenzo began without preamble, gesturing to the parchments Marco had placed on the table. "I would examine them first."

Marco slid them across without comment. Lorenzo inspected each with methodical thoroughness, his expression betraying nothing as he confirmed the authenticity of his grandfather's acknowledgment of Giovanni's parentage and the detailed account of the ritual executions.

"You understand," he finally said, looking up at Lucia, "that even if genuine, these represent actions taken by men now dead for decades. The Florence they knew no longer exists."

"Yet the power structures they created persist," Lucia countered. "Built on foundations of concealed blood and ritual murder."

Lorenzo set the documents aside carefully. "What exactly do you seek, beyond exposing ancient crimes? Florence's stability cannot withstand the public revelation of such history. Too many depend on Medici banking, Medici patronage, Medici protection from foreign interference."

"Justice takes many forms," Lucia replied, her voice steady despite the enormity of sitting face-to-face with the heir of her family's destroyer. "I have already exacted blood payments from four men who benefited directly from Vinciguerra tragedy. Your life would complete the pattern."

"Yet you're here instead of attempting to kill me," Lorenzo observed. "Why?"

Lucia's eyes flickered briefly to Isabella. "Perhaps I recognize that vengeance, once complete, leaves an emptiness no satisfaction can fill. Perhaps I've grown weary of death after forty years of nurturing its cause."

"Or perhaps," Isabella interjected gently, "you recognize that the greatest victory isn't eliminating your enemy but transforming him into an instrument of the justice you seek."

Lorenzo shot his niece a warning glance, but she continued undeterred.

"Uncle, we have an opportunity to heal wounds older than anyone in this room. Not through denial or destruction, but through acknowledgment and restoration."

"What restoration can possibly address such ancient wrongs?" Lorenzo asked skeptically.

Isabella had prepared for this question during the journey from the cathedral. "First, official acknowledgment in private family records that Giovanni de' Medici was son of Maria Vinciguerra, making her bloodline part of our legitimate heritage. Second, return of properties confiscated from the Vinciguerra estate in 1439, or their modern equivalent in value. Third, a proper memorial for the executed family members, conducted with dignity rather than secrecy."

Lorenzo's eyebrows rose at the comprehensive nature of these proposals. "You've given this considerable thought, niece."

"Someone must bridge these divided bloodlines," Isabella replied simply. "Who better than one who carries both?"

Lucia studied Isabella with newfound respect. "The properties matter little to me now. What I seek is acknowledgment—not public shame that would destabilize Florence, but private recognition that would honor those who were not just killed but erased from history."

"And the killings?" Lorenzo pressed. "Four men dead by your hand or command. Justice for them is also my responsibility."

Marco spoke for the first time since entering the palazzo. "Those debts are paid in blood already spilled. The Magnificent One lives—that is concession enough."

A tense silence filled the chamber as Lorenzo considered. Isabella could see her uncle's mind working through implications, calculating political equations no one else in Florence could fully comprehend. When he finally spoke, his voice carried the weight of decision.

"I will acknowledge the blood connection in private family records—a truth to be preserved but not proclaimed. The Vinciguerra properties—or their current value—will be restored to Lucia as sole surviving heir. A private memorial may be arranged, provided it remains exactly that: private."

He leaned forward, his gaze hardening. "In exchange, all documents suggesting ritual aspects to the executions will be surrendered and destroyed. The recent murders will be attributed to common bandits or political rivals, with no connection to Vinciguerra vengeance. And you both will depart Florence permanently, never to return during my lifetime."

Lucia nodded slowly, her life's mission suddenly transforming into unexpected compromise. "And after your death?"

"Your descendants may return, but not you," Lorenzo stipulated. "Too many know your face now, too many would question your presence. This chapter must end definitively."

"What of me?" Isabella asked, suddenly concerned about her own position in this negotiated peace. "My blood connection to the Vinciguerra remains a fact, regardless of documents preserved or destroyed."

Lorenzo turned to his niece with calculating assessment. "You have demonstrated both judgment and initiative in this matter, Isabella. Perhaps it's time your role in our family reflected these qualities."

"Meaning?" she pressed.

"You will become keeper of the family archives—all of them, including those in the secure vault. The complete history of our family, with its glory and its shadows, will be your responsibility to maintain for future generations." Lorenzo's expression softened marginally. "Your father would have approved of such a role for his daughter."

Isabella felt the weight of this responsibility settling upon her—not a burden to be escaped but a purpose to be embraced. The keeper of both bloodlines' truths, ensuring neither would again be erased from history's accounting.

"I accept," she said simply.

Lucia studied Lorenzo with the penetrating gaze of someone who had dedicated decades to understanding an enemy. "You are more practical than your grandfather, Magnifico. Cosimo would never have compromised with enemies, even in defeat."

"Florence's needs have evolved since his time," Lorenzo replied evenly. "And perhaps I recognize that some conflicts can never be truly resolved through elimination."

The bargain struck, practical details remained. Properties to be identified, documents to be exchanged, arrangements for safe passage from Florentine territory. As these negotiations proceeded with businesslike efficiency, Isabella observed the subtle recalibration occurring in all present—enemies becoming reluctant allies, vengeance transforming into resolution, the past's grip loosening enough to permit a different future.

Later that evening, after Lucia and Marco had been escorted to temporary accommodations under guard pending their departure, Isabella found herself alone with Lorenzo in the hidden archive beneath the chapel. By lamplight, they examined the family records that would now be amended to acknowledge truths concealed for generations.

"You took an extraordinary risk today," Lorenzo observed, his tone balanced between criticism and admiration. "Approaching them alone in the cathedral, offering terms without authorization."

"I saw an opportunity that formal plans couldn't accommodate," Isabella replied without apology. "Sometimes the boldest move is the safest, especially when dealing with those who expect only hostility."

Lorenzo smiled slightly—the private smile reserved for moments of genuine rather than political pleasure. "Your father had similar instincts. Giovanni could sense when convention needed to be abandoned in favor of inspiration."

Isabella felt a warm glow at this comparison. "Tell me about him—my father. Not the official history, but the man himself. Did he know of his Vinciguerra heritage?"

Lorenzo considered this as he carefully replaced a volume on its shelf. "I believe Cosimo told him when he reached maturity. Giovanni never spoke of it directly, but there were occasions when he advocated for unusual restraint in family vendettas. He would say, 'Blood feuds ultimately claim blood from both sides.' Perhaps that was his acknowledgment."

"And my mother? Did she know she was marrying a man of mixed bloodlines?"

"That I cannot say," Lorenzo admitted. "Your father guarded some privacies even from his brothers. But he loved you fiercely, Isabella. When fever took him, his last coherent words concerned your future."

This revelation touched Isabella deeply. Her father had died when she was seven—old enough to remember his kindness but too young to know him as an adult might. "What did he say?"

"That you carried the best of multiple legacies and should be educated accordingly—not just in womanly arts, but in history, politics, languages. It was his deathbed request that shaped your unusual education."

Isabella absorbed this insight with profound gratitude. Her father's influence had reached across the years, shaping her into someone capable of resolving conflicts he himself had inherited.

106

"The sixth mask," she said suddenly, remembering the mysterious reference that had haunted Lucia's journals. "Did you ever discover its significance?"

Lorenzo moved to the alcove where the original masks had once been displayed on five pedestals. He pressed a hidden mechanism, revealing a sixth pedestal concealed within the wall itself.

"According to Michelozzi, who heard it from my father, the sixth mask was created but never used," Lorenzo explained. "It was designed for Maria Vinciguerra herself, had she lived to witness her brothers' punishment. Cosimo couldn't bring himself to destroy it, yet couldn't bear to display it alongside the others. So it remained hidden, a secret within secrets."

"And now?" Isabella asked.

"Now it remains lost, taken when the others were stolen six months ago." Lorenzo closed the hidden compartment. "Perhaps that's fitting. Some ghosts are better left unconfronted."

As they completed their work in the archive, amending records to acknowledge Isabella's dual heritage, she felt a peculiar sense of completion—not just of this crisis, but of a journey of self-discovery she hadn't known she was undertaking.

"What becomes of us now, Uncle?" she asked as they prepared to ascend to the world above. "With these truths acknowledged between us, if not before Florence?"

Lorenzo considered her question with unusual thoughtfulness. "We continue building what Cosimo began—a Florence where art and learning flourish, where banking serves creation rather than merely wealth. But perhaps with greater awareness of the costs such building sometimes exacts."

"And my role as keeper of these truths?"

"Is to ensure future generations learn from our compromises, both noble and shameful," Lorenzo replied. "The Medici story includes glory and shadow. Both must be preserved if either is to be understood."

As they emerged from the hidden chamber into the chapel above, Easter evening had fallen over Florence. Through the windows, Isabella could see lights appearing across the city—homes and workshops preparing for night, the rhythm of Florentine life continuing despite the momentous revelations and negotiations that had transformed her understanding of her place within it.

In the coming days, Lucia and Marco would depart for exile in France, carrying with them Medici gold but leaving behind their most potent weapons—the documents that could have shattered Florence's fragile political balance. The four murders would be attributed to political rivalries, their theatrical elements dismissed as attempts to confuse investigation. Life would continue, power would maintain its familiar patterns, and most of Florence would never know how close the city had come to profound upheaval.

Yet something had fundamentally changed, at least within the private chambers of Medici consciousness. Isabella, now entrusted with both the glorious and shameful chapters of her family's ascent, recognized that power built on concealed foundations remained eternally vulnerable. The true strength of the Medici might lie not in what they hid but in what they dared to acknowledge—if only to themselves.

As she walked through the palazzo that evening, Isabella passed a mirror and paused, studying her reflection with new awareness. The shape of her eyes, the curve of her jaw—which features came from Medici blood, which from Vinciguerra? The question was ultimately unanswerable, the bloodlines now inseparable in her person. She was neither one nor other, but something new forged from ancient rivalries.

Perhaps that, she reflected, was Florence's destiny as well—not to choose between republic and principality, between sacred and secular, between ancient nobility and rising merchant power, but to create something uniquely Florentine from these competing influences. A city of contradictions, harmonized rather than resolved.

Outside her window, the dome of the cathedral rose against the darkening sky—Brunelleschi's impossible achievement that had forever transformed Florence's silhouette. Its construction had required both ancient knowledge and revolutionary innovation, traditional materials and unprecedented techniques. Like the city it crowned, like the family whose patronage had helped create it, like Isabella herself, the dome represented the potential of synthesis rather than elimination.

Tomorrow would bring new challenges, new negotiations, new balances to maintain. But tonight, as Florence settled into darkness beneath Easter stars, Isabella embraced her complex heritage with a sense of possibility rather than burden. The keeper of truths had found, perhaps, the most important truth of all: that understanding the past's darkness need not dim the future's light, but might instead help guide its illumination more wisely.

The Medici legacy would continue, with all its contradictions and complexities. And Isabella de' Medici—daughter of two bloodlines once locked in deadly opposition—would ensure that its full story endured, neither sanitized nor sensationalized, but preserved in the balanced measure that true history demanded.

Epilogue
Blood and Legacy

One month had passed since Easter's dramatic confrontation. Florence had returned to its rhythms—commerce in the markets, politics in the Signoria, art in the workshops scattered throughout the city. The murders that had terrorized the powerful were now attributed to a Venetian conspiracy, neatly resolved through diplomatic pressure and quiet payments. Even the interruption of Easter Mass by Savonarola had faded into anecdote rather than portent, though the Dominican friar continued his denunciations of Florentine excess from his pulpit at San Marco.

Within the Medici palazzo, subtle transformations had taken place. Isabella had assumed her new role as keeper of the family archives with dedicated purpose, spending hours cataloging and organizing the accumulated wisdom and secrets of three generations. The hidden chamber beneath the chapel had been expanded under her direction, its collection growing as she gathered scattered documents from various family properties.

On this particular morning, Isabella sat at a specially constructed desk in this underground sanctuary, carefully transcribing Cosimo's private acknowledgment of Maria Vinciguerra's son into the official family record. The original document had departed with Lucia—a concession Lorenzo had ultimately deemed necessary for final resolution—but its contents would now be preserved in Medici history, albeit in controlled form.

A soft knock at the chamber door announced Michelozzi, who entered bearing additional materials for her growing collection.

"Letters from Rome, my lady," he explained, placing a bundle of correspondence on her desk. "Exchanges between your grandfather and Cardinal Bessarion regarding the Council of Florence. Your uncle thought they should be preserved here rather than in the public archive."

Isabella nodded, setting aside her transcription. "Thank you, Michelozzi. Any word from our... relatives in France?"

The old secretary's expression remained carefully neutral. "They have established themselves in Lyon, according to our agents. The widow Vinciguerra has purchased a modest estate outside the city. Her son has taken the name Conti publicly, though they maintain their true identity in private."

"And the documents?"

"Secure in their possession, but unused. They appear to be honoring their agreement."

Isabella felt a measure of relief at this confirmation. The uneasy truce between bloodlines remained intact, at least for now.

"There is one other matter," Michelozzi added, his tone shifting slightly. "A package arrived for you personally. It bears no sender's mark, but the courier came from the direction of Lyon."

From within his robes, he produced a small parcel wrapped in plain linen and sealed with unmarked wax. Isabella accepted it with cautious curiosity, breaking the seal under Michelozzi's watchful gaze.

Inside lay a small wooden box carved with intricate precision—a Florentine craftsman's work, showing the city's skyline in miniature. A folded note accompanied it, written in an elegant hand Isabella had come to recognize from Lucia's journals.

"I shall read it privately," she told Michelozzi. "Thank you for bringing this directly to me."

The secretary hesitated, clearly torn between duty to Lorenzo and respect for Isabella's new authority. "Your uncle would wish to be informed of any communication from that quarter."

"And he shall be, once I've assessed its contents," Isabella replied firmly. "This was addressed to me, not to the Medici patriarch."

Reluctantly, Michelozzi bowed and withdrew, leaving Isabella alone with this unexpected connection to her complex heritage. When the heavy door had closed behind him, she unfolded the note and read:

Isabella,

Blood divides and blood unites, as you have learned at considerable cost. The truths you now guard shape not only your family's understanding of itself but Florence's future path. Guard them wisely, amend them honestly, and remember that history belongs not to those who make it but to those who record it.

The enclosed belonged to your grandmother Maria. It passed to me through channels too complex to explain here. Now it returns to the bloodline where both our families converge.

The sixth mask remains in my possession—not as threat but as reminder. Some histories must be preserved even when they cannot be displayed. Perhaps our descendants, meeting in some distant future beyond current grievances, will decide its final disposition.

Until that day, Lucia Vinciguerra

Isabella set the note aside and opened the wooden box. Inside, nestled on a bed of crimson silk, lay a small silver medallion bearing an unusual crest—a five-petaled lily intertwined with a falcon's talon. The Vinciguerra family emblem, she realized, modified to incorporate the Medici symbol. An ancient testament to the brief alliance between families that had produced her father.

She lifted it carefully, turning it over to discover an inscription on the reverse: *Maria to Giovanni - Two bloods, one heart. 1421.*

A gift from mother to infant son, preserved across decades of hatred and vengeance, now returned to the granddaughter who embodied that same dual heritage. Isabella felt the weight of the medallion in her palm—physically light, symbolically immense.

That evening, Isabella was summoned to Lorenzo's study, where she found her uncle in conversation with Botticelli. The celebrated painter had spread preliminary sketches across the desk—designs for a new fresco cycle commissioned for the family chapel.

"Ah, Isabella," Lorenzo greeted her with unusual warmth. "Your timing is perfect. Sandro seeks a subject that honors our family's contribution to Florence without excessive self-glorification. A delicate balance."

Botticelli bowed slightly to Isabella, his artist's eyes studying her with the same intensity he brought to all potential subjects. "I suggested the Adoration of the Magi, with Medici figures depicted as the three kings. Traditional yet meaningful."

"A subject already treated by several masters," Lorenzo noted. "Though your interpretation would undoubtedly bring fresh perspective."

Isabella approached the sketches, considering them thoughtfully. The proposed composition followed familiar arrangements—the Holy Family receiving noble visitors bearing gifts, symbolic of worldly power acknowledging divine authority.

"What if," she suggested carefully, "instead of the Magi, you depicted the Holy Family receiving all classes of Florentine society? The noble, the merchant, the craftsman, the scholar—each bringing their distinctive contributions, none elevated above the others in the composition?"

Botticelli's eyes lit with artistic inspiration. "Florence itself as a harmonious offering, with the Medici not as rulers but as participants in a collective devotion. Bold, yet humble in its assertion."

Lorenzo studied Isabella with newfound appreciation. "A composition that acknowledges our central role while emphasizing the broader community we serve. Politically astute, artistically novel."

"The strength of Florence has always been its synthesis of diverse elements," Isabella observed. "Like a family that draws vitality from varied bloodlines rather than rigid purity."

Lorenzo caught her meaning immediately, his expression flickering with momentary wariness before settling into reluctant acknowledgment. "Indeed. Diversity properly harmonized creates resilience rather than weakness."

As Botticelli began sketching this new conception with characteristic fluidity, Isabella revealed the medallion she had received that morning. "A relic of that very principle, Uncle. From our French relations."

Lorenzo examined the object with careful hands, recognizing its significance instantly. "Maria's gift to your father. I heard of its existence but never saw it." He returned it to Isabella with deliberate formality. "It belongs with you now, as keeper of our complete heritage."

This simple acknowledgment—'our complete heritage'—represented a profound shift in how Lorenzo conceptualized the

Medici legacy. No longer a narrative of pure achievement and strategic genius, but a complex tapestry that included hidden alliances, painful compromises, and blood connections once deemed better forgotten.

As Isabella departed the study later, leaving Lorenzo and Botticelli to their artistic planning, she encountered Giuliano in the corridor. Lorenzo's younger brother had been unusually subdued since Easter's confrontation, his characteristic charm muted by what they had all confronted.

"A moment, Isabella," he requested, drawing her into an alcove away from passing servants. "There's something you should know, now that you've assumed responsibility for our family's complete record."

His emphasis on 'complete' suggested knowledge of her expanded role. "What is it, Uncle?"

Giuliano glanced around before continuing in lowered tones. "Lorenzo believes the threat has ended with Lucia's departure. I'm not convinced her son shares her willingness to compromise."

"Marco agreed to the terms," Isabella pointed out. "He seemed the more pragmatic of the two."

"Perhaps too pragmatic," Giuliano countered. "During their brief stay here, I observed him closely. His hatred runs deeper than his mother's, and lacks her capacity for resolution. She witnessed the original crime as a child; he has built his entire identity around avenging it. Such purpose doesn't surrender easily to negotiated settlements."

Isabella considered this assessment thoughtfully. "You believe he might return despite their agreement?"

"I believe Florence has not seen the last of Marco Conti, whatever name he now uses." Giuliano's handsome face hardened with unusual seriousness. "Be vigilant, niece. The keeper of truths may become their defender as well."

With that cryptic warning, he continued on his way, leaving Isabella to ponder its implications. Was Giuliano's concern legitimate insight or merely residual suspicion after decades of political maneuvering? The Medici had survived through equal measures of genius and paranoia—sometimes difficult to distinguish between the two.

Later that night, as Florence slept beneath a canopy of early summer stars, Isabella stood at her chamber window overlooking the city her family had helped shape. The medallion hung around her neck now, concealed beneath her clothing but present—a physical reminder of her complex inheritance.

In her hand, she held another object—a small iron key recovered from the workshop where Lucia and Marco had planned their revenge. According to Lucia's journals, it opened a hidden compartment in the original Vinciguerra palazzo, now converted to Medici banking offices. What secrets might still remain there, overlooked during the hasty confiscation forty years earlier?

Tomorrow would bring new discoveries, new connections between past actions and present consequences. The sixth mask remained unaccounted for—a final piece of the puzzle that represented both threat and opportunity. And somewhere in France, relatives of both blood and hatred contemplated their next moves in a game spanning generations.

Florence spread before her—magnificent, contradictory, resilient. Like the family that had helped forge its Renaissance identity, the city embodied both enlightenment and shadow. Isabella's role now transcended mere record-keeping; she had become guardian of a legacy whose complete acknowledgment might prove either its salvation or its undoing.

The medallion warmed against her skin, two bloodlines symbolically reunited in its design just as they were literally reunited in her person. Whatever came next—whether continued peace or renewed conflict—Isabella de' Medici would face it with the strength drawn from finally embracing the fullness of her heritage, neither denying its darkness nor diminishing its light.

Blood had indeed called to blood across the years, as Lucia's first message had proclaimed. But perhaps that call could summon understanding as well as vengeance, recognition as well as retribution. Perhaps the true legacy of both families might yet be found not in their ancient enmity but in their reluctant reconciliation—a pattern reflected in Florence itself as it navigated between republican ideals and practical governance, between spiritual devotion and worldly achievement.

Isabella closed her window against the night air and turned to her writing desk, where her personal journal awaited. Tonight she would record these events in her own words—not the sanitized version that would enter official archives, but the complex, contradictory truth as she had experienced it. Future generations of Medici would inherit not just power and wealth, but understanding—the most valuable currency of all in a world where the past never truly released its hold on the present.

And somewhere in the shadows of that present, the sixth mask waited—final testimony to a history not yet fully resolved, a legacy not yet completely understood. The faces of retribution had revealed themselves one by one, but the face of reconciliation remained partially obscured, its features still forming in the crucible of conflicting blood and shared destiny.

Isabella dipped her pen and began to write, adding her voice to the long conversation between past and future that constituted the true strength of both her family and her city. In doing so, she claimed her place not merely as keeper of secrets but as architect of understanding—a role that transcended the limitations placed on women of her time and reached toward a wisdom that neither Medici nor Vinciguerra alone could fully comprehend.

THE END

Enjoyed this book?

Share your thoughts with a review and help more readers discover it! Your feedback truly makes a difference.

☆ ☆ ☆ ☆ ☆

To be the first to read my next book or for any suggestions about new translations, visit: https://arielsandersbooks.com/

SPECIAL BONUS

*Want this Bonus Ebook for **free**?*

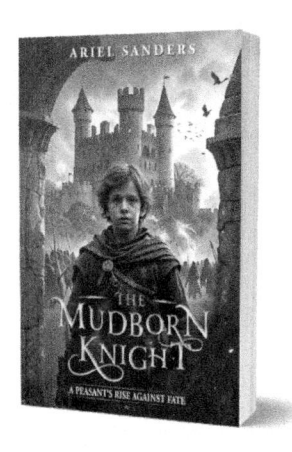

SCAN W/ YOUR CAMERA TO DOWNLOAD THE EBOOK!

SCAN ME